EVERLY TAYLOR

Just A Girl Named River (1)

To the daughters who are trying their best to be the best. And to the women that don't know what they want in life, this one's for you.

Contents

Acknowledgments

To my personal assistant Jaz, for always doing my bidding and cheering me on.

To my husband for encouraging me to follow my dreams.

To my beta and ARC readers, thank you for taking a chance on a debut author that has no idea what shes doing.

And lastly to all my new readers, thank you for taking a chance on my story and I hope you love River and the boys as much as I do.

1

Leaving

Today is the day. I have just graduated from high school and need to get away. I hug my friends and look around. I see my Grandma standing there waiting for me.

"Grandma!!!" I say, running over to her. Her smile gets huge, and she opens her arms for a hug.

"River dear, I am so proud of you." As she notices me looking around, her smile fades. "She didn't make it, dear."

"Of course she didn't make it, she never seems to make it." She, as in my Mom. Ever since my Dad died when I was ten, my Mom has wasted her life. I am not sure how she was before she and my Dad got together, but they met right before my Dad got deployed overseas. She found out she was pregnant with me while my Dad was on deployment. He was there when I was born, but he spent a lot of time deployed. My parents never married, but my Mom knew Dad could take me if she didn't act right, or at least that is what I believe. She didn't act the way she does now, and basically for the last eight years, my Grandma has taken care of me. My Mom has been hooked on drugs since the day my Dad was laid to rest. I have lost count of the number of guys she has had sex with for drugs. The last number I remember was near two hundred fifty. She can't go a single day without a fix, and has even been sent to rehab a few times. She had a baby not long ago, but the Dad's parents ended up with custody of her. She is now five, and I have yet to see her. My Dad's parents live in Italy, where my Dad was last stationed. I haven't seen them since his funeral, though we still talk once a week.

I was so disappointed that my Mom couldn't pull the needle out of her arm to come see me walk across the stage for my diploma. I knew then I had to go far, far away from her. She didn't care about me, so why should I care about her? The world couldn't be that bad, could it?

I didn't want anyone to know that I was planning on leaving, so after I had lunch with my Grandma, I went to the bank to take out my money. I withdrew all of it, and there was a lot there. My life savings. My Dad had started the account the day I was born, and it was supposed to be for college, but I am sure he would be proud if I took it to start my life, away from the woman who was destroying it. I had sewn a pocket in my bra to keep the credit card and licenses in, so I wouldn't have to carry a purse with it in, just in case it got stolen.

I managed to walk into my house, and I found my Mom in bed. She was passed out with all of her drugs lying around the bedroom, and a new guy lying next to her. I made sure to stay quiet and not wake them up because I didn't want to deal with that. I walked to my room and closed the door. I went to my closet, I opened it up, and I found my two suitcases. Between those two suitcases and my backpack, I would need to fit as much of my stuff as possible. I already knew I was going to have to put a few outfits and personal stuff in my backpack to carry with me. Even though my Mom spent all her leftover money on drugs, my grandparents always made sure I had what I needed. Along with my cell phone, laptop, and clothes.

I grabbed my laptop, makeup bag, toothbrush and toothpaste, hair brush, other personal hygiene items, along with a few changes of clothes, and stuffed them into a backpack. I would keep this with me, and when my suitcases go under the bus, I would still have these just in case. I started to pack my favorite clothes first, just in case I ran out of room. I took a little bag thing I found in the hall closet that would fit shampoo and bathroom stuff in it, and filled it up with everything important first. I stuffed my bags full and remembered I needed a few of my important documents. But I was worried about losing them or them getting stolen. I scanned them into my laptop so I would have a backup just in case, and put them all inside my backpack.

I grabbed my bags and started to hitchhike towards the Kalamazoo Greyhound bus station. After I started my long walk, a guy from my school stopped and picked me up.

Dylan was his name. "Where are you going, River, and why do you have all your bags?"

I was grateful he picked me up, but I wasn't ready to talk about my life at home, as it was something I hid from everyone. I never invited people over. My friends didn't even know where I actually lived. "Dylan, can I tell you something without you telling anyone?"

"Yeah, of course, I got your back, girl."

As far as I know, he did. Because he had become one of the best guy friends I had. I was still unsure if I should let him in or not. But knowing in a few short hours I wouldn't even be around here anyway, and he was off to college in California on a football scholarship, I would probably never see him again. "I need to go to the bus station in Kalamazoo. I have to leave, and I have to leave now before I change my mind. My Mom doesn't care about me; she never really has. She is at home right now, possibly overdosed on heroin with a new guy next to her. So I need to move, I need to go somewhere that no one even knows who River Marie Hammond is."

The look on Dylan's face proves to me that he had no clue what it was like to be an adult at the young age of ten. He just stared at me like he didn't know what to say or what to do.

"Dylan, can you drive or what?"

"Oh yeah, yeah, I got you girl…. But if I take you to the bus station, will you promise me one thing?"

"What?" I asked, worried about what he would say.

"Will you keep in touch with me? I mean, let me know you're OK. I never knew about your Mom, and now I feel horrible that I didn't take the time to learn more about you. But at least let me know you're OK, and you got to where you wanted to go?"

His request didn't seem to be that horrible of a request. So I agreed and he drove me to the bus station, which was only forty-five minutes away. When we got there, I got out and grabbed my bag, and turned to say goodbye to Dylan. He leaned over and kissed me. His lips touched mine, and sparks shot through my whole body. His tongue found its way into my mouth, and I copied what he did. It was the most magical, passionate kiss I have ever experienced. I didn't want it to end, but I didn't want to stay here, either. That was the first time Dylan had ever shown any interest like that in me. And now he's making me doubt my ideas. But I know he's leaving next week too, so it's not like it will ever even work. I pull myself away and tell him I will text him when I know where I am going or if I know where I will end up.

"River, I have always liked you, I mean like, like you. Please don't leave me hanging and worrying about you. I wish I had told you my feelings before you decided to leave me."

My heart fluttered. I smiled and promised to keep in touch. I turned and walked away. I asked the lady at the ticket booth for a ticket to anywhere but here. She looked at me like I was nuts. It made me begin to wonder if I was nuts to even think I could go somewhere and start all over.

"What are you running away from, young lady? Whatever it is, it can't be that bad."

Bah, she had no idea, I thought to myself. Maybe for her, life wasn't so bad, but for me, I had to prove to myself the world wasn't like that. The lady gave me a ticket for the bus that was boarding next. That bus was headed to Las Vegas. I paid the lady and boarded the bus. I found a seat near the middle, sat down, and pulled out my headphones. According to my ticket, I was stuck for over forty hours on this bus. This meant I would be that much further away from my Mom, and from the horrible life I had tried to shut out. The life that no one could even begin to imagine.

I was a little bit scared but a lot anxious. Many questions began to fill my head.

Will I find a job? Will I find a place to live? Do I stay in Vegas, or do I buy another ticket to nowhere?

I touched my bra and the secret pocket, assuring me I could do this and that all my stuff was still there. I looked down at my phone, and it was nearly midnight, and the bus was getting ready to leave. I knew that I had to send a text to my best friend AnnaBell and my Grandma because both of them would want to know. And it wouldn't be right to just leave and not tell them.

Text 1:

Hey AnnaB, I am on the bus and heading to Vegas. I am still a bit nervous about what is to come, and if I am making the right choice. Not sure what I am going to do when I get there, but that is the only place to go as of now. I have forty hours to make some choices. I love you and I am going to miss you. Please don't forget about me. MSU is lucky to have you as a student. <3 PS without you, my life would have been much worse than what it was, and someday I will explain everything to you as I keep promising you that. ILY

Text 2:

Hi Grandma, I know you would have tried to talk me out of going, but I had to go. I am on a bus headed to Las Vegas. I know you tried and did your best to help raise me, and without you, I wouldn't be the person I am today. I had to do this for me, Grandma, so please don't be mad at me for wanting to get away from my mother. I am not doing this to hurt you or her, but I have to do it for me. I took all the money out of my savings that I have been saving and that my Dad had saved for me to go to college, and I am using it to start my life. I love you, Grandma, and I will text you every day. I promise.

I sent both texts, not thinking I would hear anything from anyone till at least morning. When my phone vibrated. I looked down to see who it was because it surprised me. It was Dylan.

Text:

Hi River, I know I can't change your mind, and I wasn't trying to with that kiss. I have wanted to tell you how I felt for several years now. Please let me know that you're OK and if you need anything. I will come to help you if you need me, too. <3

Reply:

Dylan, I am headed towards Vegas, not sure if I will stay there. You need to go to college, and things would be complicated even if I stayed with you, going to CA. I promise, when I get to Vegas, I will let you know what I decide to do. I can't express what I feel, because right now I am unsure.

Was that the right thing to say? It's the truth. Dylan would be my choice of guys from high school, but not someone I had ever thought about dating. He has dark hair that you can run your fingers through. He was six feet one inch with a hard body of muscles that make you want to lick things off it. His eight pack is oh my, so yummy. And his dark-ish greenish eyes are to die for. He was more popular, I would say, than I was. Not that I wasn't popular, I just liked to stay out of the spotlight. Dylan loved the attention, but I didn't so much. I figured the spotlight would lead to wanting to know more about my life, and I wanted to leave that behind. I wanted all my dirty secrets to be flushed out to sea, and my way of getting rid of the past is to start new in the future.

While I was lost in thought, my phone vibrated again. This time it made me jump. I pick it up and look at it, surprised. The text message name read Grandma R. That would be Grandma Rizzo, who is my Dad's Mom. I have my Mom's last name; I was never given my Dad's last name, as my parents were never married. I was a bit surprised as I just talked to her yesterday morning before my graduation.

Text:

River dear, your Grandma just called me and to my surprise. As she doesn't normally call. She wanted me to know that you have taken all your money and are headed to Vegas. Dear, please tell Gramma that you are not going to blow all that money in the slots. And tell me what is going on, too, please, dear.

I wasn't ready to tell Gramma yet what was going on. I was going to wait. She knows about my Mom and most of the stuff that has gone on, but not everything. NO one knows everything. I had to tell her what I was doing.

Text back:

Gramma, I had to leave. I can't do it anymore. I am not going to blow my money in the slots, I need to start my own life. Daddy wouldn't want that life for me. Maybe at some point, I will end up in Italy with you. But for now, Vegas is the only bus I could board. I promise I will still have communications with you like always, maybe even more now. You wouldn't happen to know anyone who could hook me up with a room in Vegas, would you, Gramma, for a few days or weeks?

Did I mention that my Grandma R is well off and high up in the chain with lots of connections? I should have reached out to her long ago, but I was hoping my Mom would get better, or that maybe if I stayed, she would try. But I learned that is not how it works. Until she is ready to get better, she won't. And she hurt me A LOT.

I closed my eyes. I knew I was in for a long ride.

2

Bus Ride

Whoa, I must have fallen asleep as I jumped and awakened myself. I pick up my phone and see several missed messages, and the music in my headphones has stopped. Wow, it's six in the morning already. I must have needed some sleep, and never thought I would be able to sleep so heavily on the bus. And by heavily, I mean heavy enough to not even notice that someone sat down next to me. I turned and looked to see who it was. Knowing I wouldn't even know this person, but it was worth a shot to evaluate the situation.

I notice the person is wearing green Converse, male. He was wearing dark colored jeans, which I found a bit odd because it was springtime and a bit warm for pants. As I looked at my exposed legs, remembering I was still in my short lavender and white dress with a gray tie around, I wore it to graduation. I could kick myself in the ass right now for not putting on some shorts before I left home. I turned and looked at the guy's legs next to me and could tell by the fit of his jeans that he had some muscles on his legs. I began to blush a little, and I have no idea why. It's not like I am a stranger to guys or anything. I decided I would just turn and look at who was next to me, worried I might have to change seats.

When I turned, I was in total shock and surprised to find that I had a set of eyes and the most amazing, gorgeous smile staring at me. As I had been caught red-handed doing something wrong, even though I hadn't. I was lost in his eyes. They were a shade of blue that reminded me of the ocean, with a hint of green. What my friends would call bedroom eyes. Dark hair that is about five to six inches long, or so, and is a little bit messy. He still had a smile on his face when I looked at his lips, and they were perfect. I could only think, what would it be like to kiss those lips? I could feel my heart beat faster, and it felt like butterflies in my stomach. WHY, I have been around attractive guys before. I can feel my face heat up, and I am sure they have started to turn a different shade of pink or maybe even red. I'm not sure at this point. I bashfully smile and turn my head out the window.

River, what is wrong with you? Why are you acting like a twelve-year-old around this guy? I grabbed my backpack, looking for something to drink because all of a sudden, my mouth was dry. Great, I forgot to pack a couple of water bottles. I find some gum and start chewing, still trying not to look at the guy next to me. But I find myself looking again.

This time, he wasn't looking back as he was on his phone. I noticed a little bit of stubble growing back on his face, which made me think he had shaved but not within the last day or two. He had on a green American eagle shirt. It fit him so well, I could swear I could see the definition of his muscles not only in his arms but on his chest as well. I could almost feel myself drooling.

I looked back up to his face and saw he was looking at me again, and of course, my body didn't do me any good; it started to heat up again.

"Hi," he says to me, and all I can do is blush more and be at a loss for words.

"Ummm, hi," I managed to say. Good going, River. Why not make a bigger fool of yourself? How are you ever going to make it on your own if you can't even have a simple conversation with a guy? Mind you, he is the most delicious-looking man I have ever seen in my life. And just looking at him makes parts of my body tingle that I have never felt tingle before.

His smile grows even bigger than before, and good Lord, let me tell you my stomach flutters even more than it had earlier. Why was this guy making my body go all crazy like this? I have never in a zillion years felt like this. Honestly, I never thought I could.

Maybe the whole new life is the reason for this. Yes, that has to be it. It has to be the fact that I am trying to start a new life, and I am all alone, and this is a new experience, so it has to be making me feel weird inside.

"I'm Noah. And you are?"

River, pull yourself together. Breathe in, breathe out. Breathe in, breathe out. OK, now talk to the hot demigod Noah. "River, I'm River. Nice to meet you, Noah." And I managed to even smile at the end, and batted my long black eyelashes at him. There we go, girl. See, I knew you knew how to flirt. It's not like you never had any boyfriends or anything. But this guy is hotter than any other guy I have ever seen. Noah, the demigod. Noah. Yup, that name had a nice ring to it.

He is still staring at me. Do I have a booger hanging out of my nose? Why is he staring at me? I knew it, there is something wrong with me. That is why none of my other relationships ever worked out.

As he read my thoughts, he said to me, "I can't help but get lost in your beautiful eyes. I am trying to read them. They feel broken. But so hopeful. It's like you have so much to tell, yet you don't."

He is most definitely a demigod. How else would he know that?

"Are you following me, or something?" I had to ask, maybe he is one of Dylan's friends coming to spy on me. I mean, I did just tell Dylan all about my Mom. "Are you one of Dylan's friends playing some kind of prank on me?"

He looks confused. "Who is Dylan, and why would he prank you? You were already asleep on the bus when I boarded in Chicago. So I am not even sure I know where you are coming from."

Good going, River. Was my Mom high when she named me River? Why can't I have a goddess name like Athena or Gabrielle? Nope, my Mom had to name me after a body of flowing water, another great thing my Mom did for me.

"Never mind, I'm sorry. I just thought maybe this guy I went to high school with asked you to join me on this road trip." I felt bad. I was a bit paranoid, but if you grew up with my Mom, you would understand.

His phone dinged, and he looked down at it, which gave me time to check mine. I had a couple of text messages, so I decided now would be a good time to check them.

Text 1:

River, WTF? Seriously???? I mean, I would have loved a road trip to Vegas with you, even if I didn't stay. I have a month before I have to move into the dorms and start practice. I need out of this *little town, too, ya know. Anyway, I hope you have fun and don't forget about your AnnaB when you get there and start making new friends. Also, take pics of the cool stuff and send them to me. Since my lonely ass is never leaving Michigan at this rate. Best of Luck, Love.... <3 PS you better text me every day so I know you are at least alive.*

I find myself smiling at her message because she really would have come, but I was afraid she wouldn't go back. It's bad enough when we go to Grand Rapids to the club or Kalamazoo to get her to leave. She has a love for guys, and they have a love for her.

Text 2:

I understand that you wanted to let your wings spread and fly. I knew this day was going to come, and I knew that your Mom had pushed you over the edge since you had gotten older and could stand up to her and her boyfriends. I am glad you decided to leave, but I wish you had come to me before you did it so I could have helped you. But you are only young once. Before Papi passed on, he saw what your Mom was doing to you and wanted to make sure you would be alright on your own. In the front little pocket of your backpack, I put in a gift, your graduation gift from Papi and me. It's not a lot, but it will get you started in your journey. When you turn twenty-one, there will be more. Please find a job, or go to college, or something. You better text and call me every minute you get. I love you, River, and I am sorry my daughter was such a horrible mother. I did not raise her like that. You already made me proud, so make yourself proud.

I feel the tears forming and running down my cheeks, and I look for a tissue in my bag. I can't even see through the tears in my eyes, but I notice a tissue in front of my face, barely. What, how did that get there?

I turn. OMG, I forgot that the demigod of hotness was sitting next to me. I take the tissue and wipe my eyes.

"Thank you," I say to him, trying not to sob any more than I already am.

He flashes me a smile. "Wanna talk about it?"

Yes, no, I don't know what to even think right now.

"It was just a message from my Grandma. She wanted to tell me that she loves me."

OK, I lied, but is he even going to know? Yes, probably. But I don't want to go into details. He is a stranger who won't quit looking at me.

"Usually, when my Grandma tells me she loves me, I don't feel the urge to cry. I will assume there is more to this story, but I won't bug you to tell me the rest. Right now, anyway. Deal."

"Deal for what? Even if you did ask, I wouldn't tell you any more than that, I don't even know you." I replied to him.

"Well, what do you want to know? Want to play twenty questions?"

"Hmm, OK, but what my Grandma said to me is off limits."

"OK, I'll go first. Where are you coming from, River?"

"Michigan."

"Michigan? Really? I already told you I am coming from Chicago; why can't you tell me a tad bit more?"

That made me smirk. I even giggled a little. "Fine, Kalama-zoo. My turn, how old are you?"

"Twenty-one, and yourself?"

"Eighteen." I could feel myself blush. I never really flirted with a guy that was that old. I mean, I just turned eighteen this month, and the oldest guy I have ever dated was nineteen. Not that I think I will be dating this guy. But it is sort of nice to have company.

"Wow, I would have said nineteen or twenty. Where are you headed?"

Oh, what do I say? Do I tell him the truth? What if he is a crazy guy? "Vegas, at least for now. I am not sure if I am going to stay or keep on trucking away."

"Are you trying to get away from this Dylan guy?" He sounded very concerned.

"I think that would be another question, and it was my turn," I say playfully to him with a smirk.

He laughs. "Alright, my fair lady, what shall your question be?"

"Welllllllll, where are you headed?"

He smiled at me, "Vegas, just like you, darling."

"Why?"

"Now, now, now that would be another question, and it is my turn."

Great, my words come back to bite me in the butt.

"So, would you be heading to Vegas to escape this Dylan guy?" He asked me again.

I burst out in laughter. I couldn't help it. "Not a chance," I said in between laughs. When I managed to stop laughing, I was able to ask the next question. I wasn't sure if I was ready to know why he was headed to Vegas, or if he was from Vegas and in Chicago for school. So I went kind of safe, but not really. This will determine how friendly I can be. "Girlfriend, wife, or maybe a boyfriend?"

"Ummm, no boyfriend. I don't swing that way. And no wife or girlfriend. And what about you?"

"No wife or girlfriend," I reply, smiling at him and leaving it at that.

He just kept staring at me as if waiting for me to finish the response. But I don't, not right now anyway. There is nothing wrong with making him sweat. Mmmm, I wonder what the sweat would look like dripping off his chest.

River Marie, just stop those thoughts.

The silence was killing me. What do I say now? "Why are you headed to Vegas?"

"I live there. I was in Chicago on business for say. Now, do you have a boyfriend?"

I laughed a little bit, but not too loud, and I shook my head, "No, have to say I am single. Dylan isn't an ex-boyfriend." At that moment, his hand touched mine, and the bus came to a stop. I lost track of time and realized we had stopped for fuel and some food. Which I was dying for. My stomach started to growl, and I needed a couple of drinks for the next seven or so hours I would be trapped on this bus.

"We need fuel and some food, and a driver change. We will all meet back in one hour from now at 8:25. I suggest you come back around 8:15 to make sure you are here because the bus will leave without you. The bus will and I repeat will leave at 8:25 with or without you," announces the bus driver before opening the doors for everyone to pile off.

3

It Chose Me

Grabbing my backpack, I wait for my turn to get off the bus. I climb down the stairs and look around to see what is in sight. I see a McDonald's and another little restaurant, but that parking lot looks full as I am watching cars pull in and then leave again, looking for a place to park. So I decided to go to McDonald's. I start to walk towards it, thinking I will go into the gas station when I get back and grab a few things, such as water and maybe a few snacks, just in case. Looking down at what I am wearing now, I have some shorts and a t-shirt in my bag. I will change when I am done eating. Lost in my thoughts, I forgot where I was for a brief moment, or what had just happened with the demigod on the bus. When out of the blue, I feel someone grab my arm. I instinctively jump and throw a punch, connecting with the arm of the person grabbing me.

"Ouch, what was that for?"

Suddenly snapping back to reality and recognizing the voice coming from the person. Noah.

"I'm so sorry, are you OK? Didn't your Mom ever teach you

not to sneak up on someone?" Unsure of what to do, everything runs through my head quickly.

"I didn't sneak up on you. Didn't you hear me yelling for you?"

Ummm, he was yelling for me, and I didn't hear him yelling. "You never once yelled for me," I say, kind of blushing. "Did you yell for me?"

He starts laughing. "Yeah, I did. Where did you learn to do that? I mean, you didn't even look, you just swung and you hit pretty hard.... I mean for a girl that is," he says, smirking.

Oh no, he didn't. Did he really just say that? For a girl?

"I will have you know I hit hard regardless of my gender. And if you choose to classify me as a "for a girl," we will no longer need to talk. Girls are better than boys!!" I practically yell at him. I turn and storm off, leaving him standing there dumb founded.

"OK, OK, I didn't mean it like it kind of sounded. I meant most girls can't hit, and you can. But you still didn't tell me why you were so zoned out, and why you just hauled off and hit me."

I keep walking. "I'm sorry, I was thinking about what all I needed to do in the forty minutes we have." I didn't go on because the painful memories started to flood my brain.

I learned to defend myself because I had no choice. One flashback that comes to mind was when I was about fourteen and my Mom passed out from whatever drug she had decided to take. I got home after practice to find a strange, very scary-looking guy in my living room. I see he was chopping up what I assumed a line of coke, or maybe meth and turned to go to my room. I typically stayed there till her boyfriend left after they did what they wanted with my Mom. As I was walking down the hall to my room, he called out to me, but I ignored him. As I learned, it was better that way. He ended up grabbing me, telling me my Mom had a debt with him. I told him that was her problem, not mine. As he continued to pin me to the wall near a shelf of knick-knacks, I could see he wanted more than what my Mom had to offer. I reached over to this huge hummingbird rock thingy my Mom had. I kneed him in the nuts and hit him over the head with that thing. I must have hit him harder than I intended, and he fell to the ground. I took off running and didn't come back till the next day. I stayed with Grandma that night. The next day, he was gone. Now, anytime someone sneaks up on me and grabs me, I hit first and ask questions later.

But I didn't want to share that much information with this guy, I mean, what kind of freak would that make me seem? My Moms druggie boyfriends would attack me so I naturally attack first. Yeah, what a great way to start a friendship, if this is friendship.

I could tell by the way he was still walking along with me, he wanted to know about it, but did not want to push me.

"You know we have a long ride still ahead of us, do you mind if I still sit next to you?" he said, breaking the silence.

That brought my memory to the present instead of the past and made me smile. "Of course, I would rather you than some old guy."

He opens the door to the McDonald's we reached, and I go in and make my way to the counter. Not very busy here, thank goodness. I place my breakfast order and head to a table, and Noah joins me. We only had some small talk during breakfast, and it was very minimal. I finish and excuse myself to the bathroom and change into my short jean shorts and a black baby tee and freshen up a little bit. I brush my hair and teeth. I come back, and Noah's jaw drops. In turn, it makes me blush.

"Wow, I mean, Ummm..." Yup, he was lost for words.

"Well, we'd better head back towards the bus. I need to go to the gas station and grab a few things." Smiling at the result I have gotten.

We walked back quickly and quietly, though I could feel his body brushing up against mine as we walked. First, his arm brushes up against my side, then his hand brushes my hand. The hand thing felt like he was trying to decide if he should hold it or not. I would have let him, but I wasn't going to tell him that. Standing next to him, I guess him to be near six feet or even about six feet one inch. Which, to my five feet five inches height, was a tad bit taller than me. He walked with confidence, unlike me. I always just sort of walk, watching more of what's on the ground and occasionally looking at my surroundings.

As a gentleman, he opens the door to the gas station, and I go in. I go to the cooler with bottled water and grab out about four of them. I go and grab a bag of chips and a few other things. I get a couple more packs of gum to help prevent over drinking.

He chuckles as my arms are full when I make it to the counter. OK, maybe I overdid it, but it's going to be another five to eight hours till we stop again. I need to make sure. I see he only grabs a couple of waters for the ride.

"Just so you know, I am not sharing my snacks with you, so if you want a snack, you better get your own." I wanted to make sure he understood I was not going to share, and his lack of food made me worry a little bit.

"Darling, I will be fine, but since you won't share, I will grab something just in case. And because you insist on it."

Darling? Hmm, and I insisted? I don't remember insisting.

"I didn't insist on anything, just simply stating the facts. I am not sharing."

Laughing escapes his very juicy, kissable lips. Now he is laughing at me. I lick my lip and bite the lower side of it. I just want to kiss him. Would that be weird? I will wait. If, when I get to Vegas and after sitting by this guy for the next thirty-some hours, and I still want to kiss him, I will then, before we part ways. I roll my eyes and shove my stuff into my backpack. I remembered I had never texted anyone back, I grabbed my phone and looked at it, only to see that I had missed messages as well.

"Hey Noah, I am going to head to the bus. I have to send a couple of text messages real quick."

He nods at me, and I take off for the bus.

Text 1:

AnnaB, Girl, I didn't want you to come with me and like it in Vegas and not go to college. Which we both know you wouldn't want to come back, and then your parents would send the troops after you. I love you, and you will always be my number 1. Christmas break if I have a place, then we will get together out here and visit. Promise ILY

Text 2:

Grandma, I love you, and I was more worried you wouldn't want me to leave because you would want me near you, not that I wouldn't be able to make it on my own. I love you, and I miss Papi. I haven't looked yet, but thank you for the present. I will text later. I love you. And I miss you.

I read the next message: *Baby girl, where are you? You were supposed to help clean this house last night after work. It doesn't even look like you came home. Did you stay at your Grandma's?*

Great, not ready to respond to that one. I know she should be at work already anyway, and what a way for Mom to ruin my good attitude.

Next message from Grandma R: *River dear, Gramma and Poppy made a few calls, and a friend of ours has a place for you to stay. You will have to share it with their kid. The place is huge, and you will have your bedroom and bathroom. He assures me you will never even notice their kid or two coming in and out. He said they would stop by when they are passing through, but they are expecting you. There will be a key waiting for you at the Bellagio. When you get there, I will give you a number to call for a ride. Love you dear, oh, I hear that the Bellagio might even have some form of a job available, too. If not, let me know, I can help you. Safe travels, dear.*

Text back to Gramma: OMG, Gramma, you're the best. How long do I have to stay there? Will they have a way for me to find my place? I love you and Poppy.... What can you tell me about your friend's kid? Is she nice?

Too excited to even say I love you again, I hit send. I knew my Grandma would come through.

Not even much after I hit send, and she texts back like she was waiting.

Text: My dear, River, she is a great person, she is about twenty-three years young. She is a professional and works a lot, so you probably won't see much of her. She did say to make yourself at home. Remember to text when you get near a number for a car service. They will be awaiting your call and will tell the desk who you are. They will be expecting you as well. Taa taa for now dear.

I was so wrapped up in my phone, I hadn't even noticed the return of the bus driver or of Noah, who had already taken his seat next to me. I turn with a huge grin on my face.

He smiled seeing my smile, and that made my heart flutter a

little bit.

"That must have been a lot better news than the previous news you got. I like it when you smile."

Was he flirting with me? It sounds like he is flirting with me.

"Yeah, it was much better news this time, but just for the record, the news before wasn't bad, it was unexpected and not what I thought I was going to hear," I say, then try to remember if it was my turn or his in our game of twenty questions. I take a shot and decide to ask a question anyway. "So, how long have you lived in Vegas?"

He looked at me, a tad confused. Like he wasn't expecting to ask any more questions and figured maybe we're past the small talk. But yet he replies to me, "Since I was about five or six, we moved there because my Dad got a new job, and well then I found a really good job considering I am only twenty-one." He smiles as he lets me know more information about himself than I had asked. "So why don't you tell me why you chose to go to Vegas?"

Why did I choose Vegas? Up until now, I didn't know I was going to stay. Up until now, I didn't know if I would be able to stay. I hear it is busy, scary, and expensive, so until I got the message about a place to stay, I was thinking about getting another ticket to somewhere else. Or maybe even jumping the bus at one of these semi-busy towns. Maybe knowing that the demigod was going to be in the same town as me also helped.

"I didn't choose Vegas, it chose me." That is all I could say, and happy with my answer, even though it left a very confused look on Noah's face.

4

Long Day

Noah looked at me as if I were crazy, and I probably was. But at this moment, everything started to feel right. Over the next few hours, we talked about school and how he graduated from an upper-class private school with honors and even had several full-ride scholarships offered to him for college. He landed the job he has and went with it. He won't tell me what job he has. And I haven't asked. Figure he would tell me if he wanted me to know. I mean, I can't pry if I'm not willing to allow him to pry.

I told him I graduated from a little town in Michigan, with a few college acceptances that I was forced to send in by my Grandma when I knew I wasn't going to go anyway. When I was little, I dreamed of how it would be to go to college and live in a dorm, but as I got older and watched my own life go to hell, I knew then that I wouldn't want to go to college, or at least not right after high school. I told him about my Dad dying when I was little. I told him my Mom never married, which was probably better that way. I mean, come on, a guy would have divorced her so quickly with all the different men she had coming in and out of her life. I am surprised that none of the guys she already has care that she has others on the side now. Or they just don't know about it.

I found out he has brothers and sisters. I even told him I had a sister. I didn't divulge that I had never met her, but I do have a sister. I would love for one day to meet her, but I'm not even sure where to begin with that.

His phone vibrated, and he told me he needed to take care of some business stuff. I politely nodded and let him do his work. I grabbed my phone and saw no messages. Yup, feeling the love now really. Ha-ha, right, this isn't abnormal for me. I put in one earbud and turned on some music. The first song on my shuffle playlist is Eminem's "The Monster." Perfect fit for my life. That is how I feel. I wasn't sure how long it was going to take Noah to do his work, but he had his laptop out and opened some sort of map thing. It was zoomed in too far for me to notice what the map was of. I noticed what looked like a chat window open with another person. I try to look at the name without thinking I am spying on him.

Zeke, the guy's name is Zeke. I like that. I like that ring. I wonder what he looks like. River, you probably will never even meet this guy, it's someone Noah works with, and I will probably never see him after we get off the bus anyway.

I turn my attention back to my phone and check out Facebook, and notice AnnaB posted on my wall and a couple of pictures.

Facebook post on my wall: River, YOU ARE my girl, and it's only not even been a whole day since I've seen your smiling face, and I already miss you. Please promise me to never forget me. I will be there for Christmas. My Mom has already found me a ticket. Now you find me a place to come to. Much love <3 AnnaB

Aw, my bestie loves me, and now I have even more stress to figure out where I will be so she can come spend my first Christmas in Vegas with her. I have to find a job too. I click on the first pic comment. It's a pic of us at homecoming this year. We look beautiful. Her long dark hair flowing down past her butt pulled up in the front with her homecoming queen crown on and her long Princess Belle dress. She looks like a queen in that dress, and I was so jealous. She is just a beautiful butterfly with the brightest colors on her wings. With light green eyes.

Comment: Most favorite dance ever, best date with you. You were so beautiful. <3

It was she who stole the show. She was way more beautiful than I. Hello, she was the homecoming queen.

The second pic comment was on a pic of us at our state cheer competition. We were co-captains together, and we led the team to the first-ever state competition and took first place. All four years, we have been captains together.

Comment: All of our hard work paid off... We left behind the team everyone wants to be.

That was true, everyone did want to be like us. I was staring at the pics from that day when I heard Noah say something to me.

"You were a cheerleader?"

Great, more of my past being told to this guy. More ammo for him to hunt me down and hurt me. Bahaha, right, he will probably get in his fancy car and take off to tell his friends about the loser he met on the bus on the way back to Vegas.

"Yeah, Co-Captain, actually all four years while I was in high school. I shared the spot with my best friend AnnaBell."

"I wouldn't peg you to be a cheerleader, more martial arts or something along those lines. I mean, you have a mean punch and all.”

Oh, I’ll show him a mean punch. I glare at him. “Do you want to see a mean punch? Because what I did earlier wasn’t anything.”

“Oh, you are a feisty one, aren’t you?” He asked, smirking.

“Yes, yes, I am, and if you stick around, you will see a lot of it,” I replied to him. Not even thinking about it before I said it. What did I just get myself into? Insert foot into mouth. It has always gotten me into trouble.

“Challenge accepted,” he says with a huge grin on his face. *Face-palm*

Does this mean he’s going to stick around, or is he just playing mind games with me? Is he flirting? OK, this is going to drive me crazy.

“What challenge?” I mean, I don’t remember there being a challenge in my statement.

“The challenge, to see you being feisty a lot more. What does it take to get you to be feisty?”

“That! I never asked for a challenge or to have you try to make me feisty either. I was telling you I have a lot of spunk, I have been through a lot of shit and I don’t need to have some guy that is high on himself think he can make me feisty.”

Oh, viper tongue came out. I need to learn to control the way he comes out to play. This tongue has gotten me into a lot of trouble. I bite it more often and keep it at bay.

It didn’t seem to bother him at all, because he is sitting over there laughing at me like some sort of hyena. Boy, this guy is going to be hard to control. Or at least hard for me to control myself around. I can’t decide if I want to punch him in the face or if I want to jump him. He makes my emotions go all crazy. I have never in my long eighteen years of life ever felt the things

I feel when I am around this guy. I don't want him to disappear, but I don't want him staying around to push my buttons either. I had had enough of that life already.

"You know, River, I am beginning to like you. You're just the type of person I need to be around more often. You bring excitement to the boring life I have been having lately."

Huh? Can we say confused?

"How can your life be so boring? I mean, you get to go across the country for work, and I am guessing this isn't the first time you've been somewhere on a business trip. You get to see new places and meet new people along the way." I mean, really, how can that be boring? I would kill to have a job that allows me to do that.

"River, you have no clue. Just because I go to places for work doesn't mean it's fun. I meet work people. I don't get to meet people like you. Real people."

"So, you deal with fake people all day?"

Guess that was the wrong question because he laughed harder than before. Hard enough that some of the people around us started to laugh. Then he started to snort. Which in turn made me laugh, Oh Lord help me, we have a snorter.

How did I end up on this bus going to the same place as this hot guy? Not to mention someone who makes me laugh.

The rest of the afternoon flew by, and we were getting ready to stop again for food.

It gave me time to change into some PJ's since the bus was starting to get cold. I wasn't hungry, but I grabbed a sub. I was beginning to get tired, but needed to let my Grandma know I was OK. I took out my phone and sent her a text.

Text: Grandma, just letting you know I have a companion who is traveling with me. Nice guy. Don't worry, I already had to punch *him. Getting closer to Vegas, and Gramma and Poppy got me a place to stay and maybe a job. I am getting sort of tired, so I will text you in the morning. I love you, Grandma <3*

Turned off my phone and put it back in my bag just in time to have Noah settle down next to me. He, too, had put on some PJ's. His pants had Superman logos all over them. It made me smile, considering I had on Wonder Woman pants. He must have noticed because he smiled at me and I started to giggle like a little school girl.

"Superman? I would have pegged you as a Batman fan." I joked with him.

"Well, I figured you to be a Hulk fan since the green comes off you."

I ended up laughing at that. "No, I'm more like Wonder Woman or Catwoman."

I could tell he was picturing me as either one of them by the look on his face and the dirty grin he had on his. Oh! No! He better not be having dirty thoughts about me like that.

His phone rang, and it brought him out of his daydream.

"Hello," he says while he holds up his finger to let me know he has to take the call, and I just nod.

"Ummm yeah," he says. I can hear a voice on the other side, and begin to wonder if it is Zeke. "No, we are just leaving Denver, about another twelve to fifteen hours to go..... Yeah, I got it...... No...."

That is all I remember, because I was so tired and his talking soothed me and relaxed me. Even if he wasn't talking to me, I just liked to listen to him talk. I ended up falling asleep at some point in time.

5

Noah's Report

While I was on the phone talking to Zeke, I looked over and noticed that River had fallen asleep. She looks so peaceful right now. Finally, able to let her hurt leave her body. I wish she would trust me more and open up more. I can help her, and I want to help her.

I can see deep into those dark emerald eyes of hers that there is so much pain lying in the delicate body of hers. Her dark tan skin and dark hair that flows down her face look like a rose bud budding open. One that hasn't opened up yet, but is keeping all the beauty to itself. She has her head placed on my shoulder, sleeping, and this phone call took forever. I lean over and place a kiss on top of her head and tell her sweet dreams. I hold her hand and hope that maybe her pain will somehow go away.

I have not had a girl so beautiful and funny, and so fun to be around in my life in a very long time. I want this to continue. I have never had my heart flip-flops like she makes mine do.

I reach over her and take her cell phone from her bag. I program my number into her phone under Superman. And send a text to my cell and save her as My Wonder Woman. This way I can still talk to her even if things don't work out like I want them to at first, or like they are supposed to. Plans are already working into place, and I hope she doesn't hate me after the strings are pulled. I guess for now, I need some sleep.

Sweet Dreams, my Wonder Woman.

6

Welcome to Vegas

I wake to the sound of Noah talking. He must still be on the phone. I assume I had only closed my eyes and wasn't asleep all that long. I haven't opened my eyes yet, but I can feel that my head is lying on him. I don't want to open my eyes; I like knowing he doesn't seem to care that I am leaning on him. But that isn't the only thing. His hand is intertwined with mine. HE IS HOLDING MY HAND.

Don't read too much into this, River. It's not like you are "awake". Maybe you grabbed his hand while you were asleep. It could be true, but if he didn't want to hold my hand, he could have let go or moved his hand. And why is he rubbing his thumb on my thumb and along the inside of my palm? Ah, I feel the sparks shooting through my body at his touch.

I open my eyes when I hear Noah saying we were about two hours from Vegas to whomever he was talking to. Wide-eyed, I stare at him with a very confused look on my face.

He smiles. "Zeke, I gotta go. River just woke up and is looking a bit confused..... Yeah, I know..... Yup.... I said I've got to go." He hangs up the phone and turns to me. "Good Morning,

Beautiful. You missed our stop for breakfast. I hope you don't mind; I grabbed you a cinnamon roll from Burger King. I also got you a bottle of water."

"What do you mean we only have about two hours till Vegas?"

"We just passed a sign reading St. George, Utah, and that is just under two hours from Vegas."

"Thank you for breakfast," I say as I grab the food from him and remember I have to send my Gramma a message for a ride. I also look down at my PJ's and know I need to change out of them before I get to Vegas. I think Noah sees me looking at my attire and knows what I'm thinking.

"Hun, eat your food, I will block the view on this side so you can change when you're done eating. I should have woken you up. I am sorry."

First beautiful, and now Hun?! What does this mean?

I pull out my phone and turn it on while I work on eating.

There is a text message from my Grandma that I read while I am eating.

Text message: River, that is great. Maybe you have love on the way to Vegas. Let me know when you get there, as I am sure it won't be long after you awake. I love you.

Reply: I don't know about love, but I sure have sparks. <3 we'll be in Vegas in less than two hours, love you too, Grandma...

Text to Gramma: Gramma, I'm less than two hours from Vegas, and you told me to message when I got close. I can't tell you how much all this means to me, Gramma. Tell Poppy I love him too.

I look around and see that the bus is a lot less crowded than I had remembered it.

"Ummm, where did everyone go?"

Noah shrugs as he doesn't know. "They didn't get back on the bus at the last stop. The bus driver wouldn't wait. Now grab some shorts, and I'll turn my back to you and stand so you can change out of your PJ's."

When he stood up, I quickly changed. "Done."

"That was quick," he states as he sits back down, turning to me with a grin. "How did you sleep?"

"Good, since I slept through our last stop," I say, giggling.

"Yes, that you did," he says back to me. I begin to wonder how much he has slept since he had been on the phone when I fell asleep, and was on when I got up.

"Did that conference call take you all night?"

"No, I fell asleep for a little while. But I get today off, sort of."

"Sort of?" What the heck does sort of mean when it comes to work? You either have to work or you don't.

He chuckles. "It's kind of hard to explain. I have a few things I have to do, but I can do them from home. I don't have to go to work today or tomorrow."

"Maybe you can show me around?" Damn, my viper tongue came out to play. What the heck, tongue? My heart cannot take being hurt or let down, and there you go trying to make it happen.

His juicy lips turn into an ear-to-ear grin as if I've just made his day. Just then, a ping on my phone goes off.

Text message from Gramma: My darling River. I have called the Presidential Limousine in Vegas, called them at this number, 702-438-5466, and tell them you are Charlie Rizzo's granddaughter, and they will meet you at the bus station. They are awaiting your call, and they know where to take you. If you need a ride anywhere, they will be at your beck and call. No need to pay. I've already taken care of it. Love you, darling.

As I was reading the message, Noah interlocked his hand

with mine.

"Um, I have to call this limo service with a time to pick me up at the bus station."

He smiles, "About noon."

Not wanting to remove my hand from him, I start dialing the number with one hand so I can call. The line rings, and some lady picks up on the other side.

"Hello, and thanks for calling Las Vegas Best Limo service. My name is Rhonda. How can I help you?"

Best limo service? "Hi, this is Charlie Rizzo's granddaughter, River. I was told to call you and tell you a time. I will be at the Greyhound station at roughly noon."

"Yes, River, I have been waiting for your call. Roberto will be picking you up. He will have a sign with your name on it. Please look for him, and he will take you to the Bellagio. Will you need service after check-in? Just let him know. You can always call this number about fifteen minutes before needing a ride, and I will send him right over for you. Thank you for choosing us, and tell Mrs. Rizzo we do appreciate her continued service with us. Please enjoy the rest of your ride here, and I hope your stay in Las Vegas is one that you will always remember."

"Thank you, Rhonda. I will let my Grandma know what you said and look forward to having you drive me around." I'm a tad bit surprised that she said to use the service. I didn't even know my Grandma had been to Vegas.

"Is everything alright?" Noah asks me.

"Yeah, I just never knew my Grandma had been to Vegas."

I quickly got into my bag and pulled out my toothbrush, and began brushing my teeth, spitting into an empty water bottle. I run a brush through my hair and pull it up into a ponytail. I need to shower so badly, and that is going to be the first thing I do when I get to my hotel room.

I put all my things back into my backpack, getting anxious waiting, and I think Noah can tell because I'm getting a little bit fidgety.

"Why don't you listen to some music and calm your nerves since you seem so uncertain about everything?"

Aw, he noticed something about me. He can tell that I am uncertain. This is a huge jump in my life. Is it the right one? I am not even sure if it is the right choice or not. Too many things are going through my head right now. But Noah is right, maybe some music would help, and since he is back on the phone again, why not calm my nerves now?

I pick up my phone to leave the one closest to Noah out, just in case he starts to talk to me. I turned on a local band from back home called Pass of Aggression (well, that is their new name, but the song I am listening to was written when they were still known as Vintage). I lose myself in the song because it reminds me of me; the things I have gone through in my life, and whatnot. The song is called Empathy.

Lyrics:

I just let my emotions go, no one can hear me, though. Pissed at every asshole that I never know, hate the world just for being cold and I HATE myself even more for what I done before. Picturing you looking down on me, you're telling me I'm not as good as I can be. Just let me be myself, quit crowding me.

I notice that Noah is staring at my phone, at the picture that is on it. The cover of the album. Pink lips with their mouth open, holding a piece of clear light blue candy in their teeth. On the bottom lip, there is a barcode with Efxor in it. Vintage on top of the cover. I can tell he has never heard of this band, as they are local to my area.

"What?" I ask him.

"What are you listening to?" he asks me with a very confused look on his face.

I explained how I knew the band. I had seen them at least a dozen times at the Intersection in Grand Rapids. I tell him they are a lot like Rage Against the Machine. I knew the guys in the band, and they are all awesome people. He listens to them on my earbuds, and he seems to like them.

I noticed that it's almost noon, and we have spent the last hour listening to different types of music. We've talked about music, and we've found out that our playlist consists of a wide variety of music. I take the earbuds and put them in my backpack, and grab them as we pull into the bus station.

We all got off the bus. And I look around as the suitcases are being loaded onto the sidewalk. I walk over to mine and grab them. I feel a hand grab mine, and I go to swing, but I don't make contact with anyone.

"Nice try, but I was expecting it this time," I hear Noah laughing behind me.

"What the hell are you doing?"

"Helping you with your bags. I will walk with you to make sure you get to your car alright. I mean, if that is fine with you, that is?"

I smile, like I would say no to him walking me to my car. I would be ecstatic to have him walk me to my car. Nervously, I replied to him that it would be all right. He takes my suitcase in one hand and grabs my other hand and holds it inside his. He walks me out to the front of the Greyhound station, and I scan the parking lot for a guy holding a sign with my name.

I only find a guy holding a sign that reads Ms. Rizzo. I am guessing that this is the guy who is picking me up.

"Noah, I think that's the guy giving me a ride." I point to this tall guy with dark skin, short dark hair, wearing a suit. He was standing there next to a Hummer extended limo.

Noah's eyes got huge, like he wasn't expecting that this was my ride. We walked up to the guy standing there.

"Hello, ma'am. Are you Ms. Rizzo?"

"I'm River Hammond, but my grandmother is Charlie Rizzo."

"Yes, Mrs. Rizzo. She is such a sweet lady. I have orders to take you to the Bellagio. Get in, let me take your bags and put them in the trunk." He grabs my bags and opens the door to the back of the limo.

I turn to Noah to say goodbye to him. "I had a wonderful time riding with you on the bus. I am glad that I spent it with you and not some old guy. Or with a Mom and a crying baby."

He chuckles at the last comment. "River, the pleasure is all mine. I am glad that I sat next to you while you were sleeping." He bent down and kissed me on my cheek and shooed me into the back of the limo.

He only kissed me on my cheek and then practically pushed me into the limo. I knew he didn't like me, and I'd been wrong to allow my heart to try and overtake my brain. I climb in. He smiles at me and closes the door, and turns to talk to the driver before he walks away. Will I ever hear from him again?

The driver climbs in and turns to me. "Any other places you want to go today, Ms. Rizzo?"

"I am not Ms. Rizzo. Rizzo was my Dad's name, but I have my Mom's last name. I want to shower, but I don't think I'm up for anything else. At least not right now. Thank you. Can you just call me River?"

He laughs at me. "Ms. Rizzo, I will be available if you need a ride anywhere else today." He pulls out and heads south, from what I can tell.

I look around, and it's not like what the movies show. I mean, no lights and stuff. Then I remember that it is daytime, so why would there be a ton of lights? We pull into an area of town that is so busy that I can barely see the road in front of me. I'm so amused that I don't see that we are pulling into the hotel. I'm lost in the scenery when we pull up and park.

7

Rosalie's Report

Where can the little bitch be? She hasn't been home in like forever. Mom said she hasn't seen her since graduation. She said she took her to lunch after graduation, and that was it. I hope Roman hasn't gotten hold of her.

Pacing back and forth, I pick up the phone. Still no text message from her.

Text: River, listen, I need to know if you're OK. Just respond to me. I am worried. This house is trashed, and you need to come home.

As I send it, I hear a knock at the door, and then it opens. I walk to the living room to see Roman standing there.

"Where is she?" I yell at him.

"What the fuck you talking about, bitch. I want my money. You said after your little bitch graduated, you would have my money. Now where the fuck is it."

"River is missing. I can't get the money without her. You took her; I know you did."

"I didn't fucking take your bitch." He walks over and slaps me across the face. "Now I warned you, I will collect one way or another." He turns and walks away. "One week, Rosalie, or I will come back and take what is mine." He tosses down a baggie with some heroin in it and leaves.

I start crying. I open the baggie and start to liquefy the contents and put them in a syringe. Before the high gets too intense, I send River another message.

Text: Please, River. I need you... Don't let me die like this.

8

Hotel

Roberto gets out, goes around, and opens my door. "Ms. Rizzo," he says, waving his hand to show me to get out. I start to step out, and I am totally in awe. I have never seen a building so huge. A big pond out in front of the hotel, and across the street, I can see the Eiffel Tower. I never thought I would see the Eiffel Tower; I mean, it's not the one in Paris, but this is awesome. As I am standing there with my mouth dropped open, taking it all in, Roberto must have gone around to the trunk to get my bags. I turned around and reached into the limo. I spin around and see a ton of people moving around so quickly.

"Ms. Rizzo, the check-in desk is expecting you," he says, bringing me back down to earth. He hands me a card with a few phone numbers on it. "The top number is the main office line, the bottom is my private number. When you need a ride, call either one. After four pm, call the private number. Enjoy your night, Ms. Rizzo." He turns, closes the door, goes around the limo and climbs in, and pulls away. Leaving me standing there on the curb at the Bellagio.

I snap out of my trance and walk into the hotel. I was even

more in awe when I walked into the lobby. Beautiful marble floors, very colorful jellyfish-looking things on the ceiling. This place is gorgeous. I have never seen anything so beautiful. Lots of people come and go. I made my way up to the counter.

"May I help you?" the lady at the counter said sort of rudely. Like I wasn't good enough to be coming to such a nice place. She looked at what I was wearing, and her nose turned up. I looked at her. Perfect skin tone and her hair pulled up into a bun, she looks to be in her twenties. The name tag says her name is Tina.

"Hi, umm, Tina. I am River Hammond. My grandmother, Charlie Rizzo, told me to come to the counter and tell you that I am her granddaughter, and you would know what to do."

She started to laugh hard and uncontrollably. The manager walked over and looked at me, and then at her.

"Tina, we don't laugh like that at customers." Double checking me out and saying it like he is trying to be nice.

"No, no (while still laughing), you have to hear this. She says she is Mrs. Rizzo's granddaughter." Laughing even harder than before.

I am uncertain why she is laughing so hard, or what is very funny about me being the granddaughter, "MRS. RIZZO."

The manager that I have now had time to look at has blond hair and blue eyes. Young, I am thinking younger than Tina, with glasses on his face. Not bad looking in a geeky sort of way. He reminds me of Harry Potter, but much sexier and a bit hotter and with blond hair instead of dark hair. If that even makes sense. I look at his name tag, and his name is Cain. He looked at me, then started to type something on the computer. "Tina, I think it's time for you to go home," dismissing her from her duties.

"I just got here." She stops laughing to say back to Cain with a very surprised face.

"I know. Good day, Tina."

She turns and storms off, stomping like a little kid.

"I am sorry about that," Cain says to me while still typing into the computer. "I'm Cain, and if there is anything I can do for you, just let me know." He turns and hands me a key and an envelope.

I take those from him and go to open the envelope, but Cain stops me.

"No, Mrs. Rizzo says that is for you to read once you're inside the suite. Now follow me. I will show you where you are staying."

The bellhop comes and grabs my bags as I turn and follow Cain.

"When you get to where we are going," Cain started explaining, "it's like a mini apartment. First, a couple of doors to the right are the salon and workout areas. Feel free to explore them if you wish to. The first main door that has a long hall off the foyer is one of the bedrooms, but not yours. You will go into the living area, and there will be another long hall across from there. There will be a door and a hallway. That, Ms. Rizzo, will be your bedroom. On the other end of the suite will be another door with a hallway that leads to another bedroom. That is for extra guests who come and go. Feel free to the rest of the suite, just not the two extra bedrooms." He paused and opened the door to the room, and the bellhop walked in first.

Cain turns and smiles at me. What is it with this town and hot guys? I can feel my cheeks heating up while I'm standing here.

"Now there is food and stuff in the kitchen, but if you need anything to eat, feel free to order room service. If you need anything else, call the front desk and ask for me." He walks me into the foyer of the hotel room.

Oh. My. Goodness. The hotel is more like a mansion. I mean, really. The foyer is bigger than the room I had back home. I couldn't take my eyes off the beautiful things in the room. Marble floors. There is a cool chandelier hanging from the ceiling above the table in the foyer. Sure enough, off to the right are two chairs and sinks like a salon would have. I'm surprised there isn't a barber there already. Right beyond that is a workout room, I guess what you would call it. I think Cain could see the surprise in my eyes as I just stood there and stared, and didn't even walk into the hotel room.

"Ms. Rizzo, why don't you step in, and I will walk you around."

I turned and looked at him and the bellhop as they were staring at me. It made me a little bit embarrassed. I stepped in, and the bellhop grabbed my backpack and walked away.

"Come follow me." Cain walks into the workout room and through it. "There is a shower in here so you can shower if you need to afterwards, and a steam room."

Which was on the other side of the room. Wow, I never thought a hotel room would be like this. My only experience with a hotel room was at Motel 8 or something like that, with two double beds and a TV. Not a workout room and a steam room!

Right next to that, he pointed to the door that was closed and told me that the room was off-limits. He also showed me a half bath as we walked past another room that he stopped at.

"This is the dining room, and that door on the other side is a kitchen. We can have a chef come down if you want, or you can help yourself to anything that is in there."

The dining room didn't look like a dining room, it looked more like a conference room to me. It had a long table and business-looking chairs, like the ones that you see at a desk in an office. It also had a flat screen TV on the wall. I didn't walk to the kitchen, Cain didn't go in, and I figured I could check it out later. We continued to walk into a living area that had a couple of couches, a couple of chairs that were kind of a round table, and a fireplace. On the other side of the room, it also had a bar with bar stools around it.

"TV has cable, and there is Wi-Fi for your computer. The password is in that envelope. The bar is fully stocked, but I do know you're not old enough to drink." He winks at me. In a flirty way, I do believe, or in a way that he knows and doesn't care, that is why he made it a point to tell me it was there.

He walked over to the sliding doors and opened them. "This is a pool, private for you to use whenever, and a hot tub as well."

I walked over and looked outside, and there was even a fountain of a lady, and an area to hang out at with grass. I can't wait for AnnaB to see this. I have to pull my weight so I can stay here. It's like a backyard at a house, but prettier. It's bigger than my yard back home. I had a tiny house on a tiny lot, and this is bigger than my house and my Grandma's house as well. I could even see the Eiffel Tower from out there, too.

Cain walks back in and just stares at me. I can feel his eyes on me, and I turn around. He looks very serious, but very calm. "Come this way," he waves to me.

I follow him and he takes me to a door. "This is your suite. You should find what you need. If you don't, please call me. I will see myself out and allow you to get settled. Mrs. Rizzo has had a few things delivered for you as well. She also ordered lunch to be served in one hour. She said you would need some time to adjust before you eat. She ordered you a pizza. Hope that will do."

Boy, my Gramma sure does know how much I love pizza. "Thanks, but are you sure this is my room? I don't remember my Grandma saying it was going to be a house." I am still a little confused as to how this has happened.

"Yes, Ms. Rizzo, this is right. This is the room," he said, turning back to me with a cheesy grin.

That made me smile, but not because of the grandiosity of the hotel, but because of the way he looked standing there.

"Cain, will you please not call me Ms. Rizzo? My last name is Hammond, and I would rather you call me River."

"Enjoy your afternoon adjusting, River. I'd better get back to work." He says as he turns and sees himself out.

OK, River, let's go into my bedroom and get some clean clothes and open this letter. I open the door and find a hallway. There is a table sitting there with fresh-cut flowers and a card. I walk over and pick it up. Enjoy your stay. Glad to have a girl roommate, FINALLY! <3 KK

KK? I wonder if that is the daughter of the person who is friends with Grandma.

There are three doors in this hallway. I thought this was supposed to be my bedroom. I walk to the first door and I open it. It's a bathroom. Huge bathroom. I walk in, and there is a wall of mirrors and doors. I open it and it is fully stocked with towels and a closet. There is a huge walk-in shower that is bigger than the closet I had at home. There was a little closet area that had a toilet in it. Beautiful marble sink. Wow, I like this bathroom.

I walk out and head to the next door, I am beginning to

wonder what the heck it could be. Bath, and bed, but a third door? I opened it to find another bathroom. What?! Two bathrooms. This one had a walk-in closet, a soaker tub, and a vanity to do makeup with a chair. Same marble vanity and sink. Wow. But I don't need two bathrooms. I mean, I can't pee in both toilets at the same time. This bathroom lacked a shower, while the other one lacked a tub. Couldn't they just combine the two bathrooms and make one?

I open up the third door and find a huge king-size bed and flat screen TV, a dresser, a desk, and nightstands. But that is not what has me standing there with my mouth dropped open, it's the bags on the bed that do. My Gramma had clothes delivered. I walk over to the bed and find Victoria's Secret bags with all kinds of panties and bras, and they are the right size, too. Wow, how did she know? I find clothes from stores I have never heard of. Nice business suits, jeans, tee shirts, and even several bathing suits. Also, shoes, boots, and jewelry. In one bag, I even found sunglasses and purses. I don't understand how all this has happened.

Still in awe, I go to send a text to Gramma and AnnaB with pics of this place and find my phone dead. I get out the charger, plug it in, and decide to shower. I figured I should hurry since pizza is on the way.

I go through the bags of stuff Gramma got me and find a pair of jean shorts and a tank top, and decide to put those over this really cute black and white bikini. I want to swim later and sunbathe. Today I will relax and adjust, tomorrow I will look for a job.

As I go to get in the shower, I see the envelope that I had set down on the desk. I walk over to it, pick it up, and open it.

Letter:

Dear River,

I know that if you are reading this letter that I have passed on to the other world. I tried everything I could to help your Mom when I was still alive. You meant everything to me, and that is why I had the account set up for you. It was more to help your Mom take care of you. I know you always thought I was in the service, but the truth is I was not in the service. I was working undercover when I met your Mom. She had been messed up with some horrible men. Got herself into trouble, and I had to help pull her out. While I was alive, I could protect her from one of the biggest drug lords I have ever dealt with. You were her protection as my child. I know this is going to sound worse than it is, but I was working to bring this drug lord down. I was the good guy, but no one knew about my work, except for Gramma and Poppy. I have a trust fund that has been set up for you. You are now entitled to part of that. Over the next few weeks or months, you will have a lot of your life changed. Please listen to Gramma and Poppy as they will start to explain things to you. I will always love you. If the drug lord comes after you, then you need to let Gramma and Poppy know. I love you, River. I am watching over you as you are reading this letter. I wish I were standing there instead of being there in spirit. Push through this.

Love,

Daddy

I start crying. My life wasn't what I had thought it was. Drug Lord? Undercover? Too many questions, and nowhere to get answers.

I walk to the bathroom and turn on the hot water as hot as I can stand it, and climb in and hope that I can wash away the confusion in my head.

9

Reality

I stay in the tub for what seems like forever, and my fingers are wrinkling up. I know I should probably get out and get dressed. But I don't want to. I toss the idea around of staying in there even longer or getting out for a bit longer. I decided to get out. I step out of the tub and find a towel for my hair, and when I pick it up, it's warm. What? Heated towels, too. How can I be so lucky? I wrap up in a towel and walk over to the mirror. I can see the dried tear marks on my face. My whole life has been a lie. And now I'm here, starting over from the horrible life I have been living, and have no idea what is true or not. I grab the robe I found in the closet and walk back to my bedroom.

I looked at the desk where the letter was left. I walked back over to it and picked it up to find another letter and a credit card. How did I miss this? I also remembered the stuff in my bra that I needed to get out and figure out where to put it till I could go to the bank. I scan the bedroom and find that the nightstand next to the bed has a drawer. I figure this will work for the night, and I will need to get a safe or lock box for the important documents. I stick my credit card, money, and the driver's license from my bra into the stand, along with the credit card I just found on the desk.

I decided to wait to read the letter because I cannot take any more unexpected news. I walk over and grab my backpack and take out my laptop and plug it in, and set it on the desk. It needs time to charge. I turn and walk out of my room to a very quiet living space. I walked over to the bar and looked to see what was in it, needing some water and not finding any in there. I go back to where Cain said the kitchen was and walk into the conference looking dining room and see pizza sitting there. Oh, I forgot I was getting pizza. Next to the pizza was a bottle of water. I looked at it for a minute, wondering how someone put it there and who had been in here.

Note to self: ask Cain about this later. Do I need to worry about someone just coming in here? Is this kind of scary?

I sat down to eat, and while I was eating, I remember I hadn't put on any clothes, and I was still in the robe I found in the bathroom. I surely hope no one comes while I'm sitting here half-naked. That won't be a very good impression to give them. I decided to grab the food and head back to my bedroom just in case. I mean, someone did bring in food.

That made me take a quick peek into the kitchen to see if someone was still in there. Nope, but it's tiny compared to the rest of the hotel room. I took a quick scan of the rest of the hotel room, minus the two bedrooms that are off limits, and didn't see anything out of place. So I take my food and head to my room.

I open the door and hear my phone going off. I ran to pick it up.

"Hello," I say into it without even seeing who is calling.

"River, where are you?"

Great, just who I didn't want to talk to. "Mom, I can't talk right now." I set my pizza down and went to hang up the phone.

"Wait! River, did Roman take you? I need you. Help me."

Roman, who is Roman, and why would he take me? This is the first time I have ever heard my Mom say Help me with that sacred sound in her voice.

"Mom, I'm not in Michigan anymore." I hear a click on her side of the phone.

I stare at the deadline of the phone, wondering what the heck just happened. I can't pull my eyes off the phone to pull myself together.

Who is this Roman guy?

When I snap back to reality, I notice all kinds of text messages. I scarf down my food and read my messages.

Text 1: River, where are you, and how come you're not messaging me back?

Text 2: I hope you arrive safely in Vegas. Girl, I miss you. You haven't texted me back in like foreverrrr. You said you would stay in touch with me. I miss you. Love you <3 AnnaB

Both are from AnnaB.

Text Back: AnnaB, I miss you too, girl. I made it to Vegas, and I have a ton of stuff to tell you. Way more than I can tell you via text message. I love you. I cannot wait for you to come visit. <3 River

I attached a pic of the bed full of stuff, and it shows the whole room.

Text 3: River, have you made it? What about those sparks? :D
Leave it to Grandma.

Text 4: River, listen, I need to know if you're OK. Just respond to me. I am worried. This house is trashed, and you need to come home.

Text 5: Please, River. I need you... Don't let me die like this.

Those were both from my Mom.

Text 6: River, dear, text me when you're ready to talk. I hope you're not in too much shock. Poppy and I love you, and so did your Dad.

I decided to wait to text Gramma back.

Text back to Grandma: I made it, sorry my phone died and had to let it charge. THIS PLACE IS AWESOME, GRANDMA. I don't know about sparks. Sparks for me, but not for him. I love you, and Mom needs you. Well, she needs me, but I'm not there, so she needs you. I don't want to send you there, but something weird is going on. I got a text message and a phone call from her. Something about a guy named Roman and how she's going to die. Something doesn't feel right. Please go make sure she hasn't overdosed again. Please? Love you, Grandma!

I attach a pic of me in my robe and with the bedroom in the background so she can see that I am OK.

Text to Mom: Who is Roman, and why are you going to die? MOM, WHAT THE HECK IS GOING ON? ARE YOU OK?

I set my phone down. I pulled out a bra and some panties. Laughing. Leave it to Gramma to find matching cheeky panties and a bra. Cute. They are a bright pink with stars on them. These will work. I slip into them and grab up the jean shorts I was going to put on and the tank top. It's a bright green color and it looks good on me. I brush out my hair and then sit down at the laptop I had plugged in earlier.

After sitting there for an hour staring at the screen that was not turned on and not thinking about anything, I decided I should read the other letter.

River,

There is a credit card enclosed with this letter. It is your trust fund, your Dad had set up for you. You will find that anything you could need this card will cover it. Also, a letter from your Dad. I know he touches on his past with you in that letter, and now I am going to give you a few additional details. Your Dad had been working on a case to bring down a drug lord named Roman Romiraz. We believe it was Roman who killed your Dad. But we do not have proof. Stay in the hotel as long as you need. I understand you will need some adjusting time, so take it before we talk. We love you, River. If you have questions, please call, text, email, or write a letter. KK will be home sometime next week. Jazmine is one of her friends, and she may drop in and stay as well.

Much Love,

Gramma and Poppy

PS password to the Wi-Fi is beautifulswan1

I hadn't even noticed that I had been crying. I wonder if this Roman Romiraz is the same Roman Mom asked me about. Why hasn't anyone told me this before now? I am so confused. I don't even know where to begin or what questions to ask. Or who to even trust anymore.

I get a ping on my phone.

Text: River, I am not going to keep bailing your Mom out of her troubles. But I did go there and found her passed out from her drugs, so I let her be. I will try and catch her when she is not high. Honey, how is Vegas, and what do you mean, no sparks from him? He would be stupid not to have sparks. Look at you! It would be his loss if he passed you by. Love Grandma.

Grandma's text makes me laugh. She always has a way to lighten up the mood, even with the bad news about Mom. I am still worried about her, but Grandma is right, we don't need to keep bailing her out of everything.

I probably should let Gramma know I made it to Vegas and

that I am OK.

Text: Gramma, I love you. This is a lot of information to process. In time, I will possibly be able to come to terms with it. Anyway, for the time being, what bank is the credit card from, and how can I check my balance? I have a ton of questions, like could Roman still be after me or my Mom? Why didn't you tell me about this beforehand? What else do I need to know? Am I safe? I feel betrayed and uncertain of who I can trust anymore.

I started pacing, due to unresolved questions and uncertain who to ask about them. Which made me decide to put away my belongings. I figured this would help clear my mind. I sort through all of the clothes and bags on the bed. I found it to be very relaxing as I hung up shirts and pants. I found dresses already in the closet when I opened it up. All kinds, from cute little short ones to sundresses to formal wear. Which made me laugh cause who would want to take me out to somewhere formal enough for these dresses? I walk to the dresser and fill it up with the underclothes, shorts, tank tops, and bathing suits. Find shelves for shoes and purses. I lay out the jewelry on the dresser. Not a lot of it, just a few pairs of earrings, necklaces, and bracelets. I'm still in awe because this is so much stuff. I have never dreamed of this.

The phone in the bedroom rings and makes me jump. I rush over and pick it up.

"Hello," I said into the phone. Who has my number?

"Hi, Ms. Rizzo?" I could tell it was Cain from the front desk.

"River, please. Yes, it's River."

He chuckles, "Yes, River. I am sorry. But, Roberto is here and he says he has to take you for dinner. You have been requested for dinner."

Dinner by whom? Even Cain seemed a bit confused, "Who

would be requesting me for dinner. I haven't even been in town for a day, and I don't even know anyone." I asked on the phone. "Where are we going, and what do I wear? And who am I having dinner with?"

After I said who am I having dinner with again, I knew I had been repetitive, but I wanted to know who.

"Ms. Rizzo, um, I mean River, Roberto says to have you wear a casual dress. Will not say with whom you will be meeting for dinner. How long till you're ready so I can let him know?"

"Um," lost for words or time, I have to think because um is not the response he needs. Come on, River, think. "Give me about half an hour." I think I have to rush and get dressed, brush my teeth, and make up? Do I put on makeup? But who am I meeting?

"Roberto said perfectly, he will meet you outside your room." Cain hangs up, and I run to the closet.

I pulled out a white top and red bottom dress. The dress has a little design on the top and a flowing bottom. No sleeves, and short but not slutty short. I found red velvet shoes to match and a hand wallet that is the same red. Perfect. I walked over to the dresser and put on red ruby earrings and a diamond ring. I found a necklace that looks like a bow with a diamond in it. I have never felt so pretty before. I run a brush through my hair and throw on eyeliner and mascara. I don't want to be too anxious, but I am. Who am I meeting? I grab some money and put it in my wallet, pick up my phone, and put it into my bra. Since I do not have a purse, I don't want to lose it and head to the door.

I walk out of the building and find Roberto standing there with the door open on the limo. I walk over to him.

"Your ride awaits you, Ms. Rizzo."

UGH, seriously, Roberto?

"Um, River, remember," trying to correct him. But he just laughed, and I climbed into the back. He shuts the door and climbs in. I lean up and say to him, "Do you know who I am meeting or where we are going?"

He turned to me, "Ms. Rizzo, I am told to just tell you to sit back and enjoy the ride." He gets a big grin on his face and turns to drive.

I throw myself back and let out the air. I blow out the air hard enough that I can feel the hair that is dangling in my face move. Won't someone tell me what is going on?

10

Grandma's Report

I get a text about Roman and rush over to see if Rosalie is OK. Of course, I found her passed out on the floor next to her bed with a needle still in her arm. What am I going to do? She has been like this since she was sixteen. She is so thin and needs to eat. She is going to end up dead if she doesn't change, and poor River had thought she had died a couple of times before. No daughter needed to see their mother the way River has had to see her Mom. If it wasn't for me, River would have ended up in foster care.

I took the needle out of her arm and tossed it in the trash. Gather up my keys and head back home. I have several hours before she wakes up. Which gives me time to make a very, very important phone call.

"Hello, it's Elenora. I need to speak with you about Rosalie and River. Yup. Roman is back. River mentioned him in a text message and said that her Mom mentioned him too. We need to defuse this situation, but Rosalie is high, possibly overdosing. I am not sure where or what to do about this. Can you help, or do you have a plan? Yes, Ma'am, I understand. Thank you."

Now all I can do is wait.

11

Gift From Dad

I sit waiting patiently as Roberto drives out of town a little way, trying to figure out who could even possibly want to have dinner with me. I mean, no one even knows where I am except Noah, AnnaB, and family. I know my family and AnnaB aren't here. Noah? Could Noah want to meet me? Why couldn't he just call me? Wait, he doesn't even have my number, so how could he call me? But if he managed to do this? Couldn't he just call the hotel and ask for me? I mean, he knew where I was going, and how could he have made these arrangements? So many thoughts were running through my head that I wasn't even paying attention to where we were going, and next thing I knew, we were pulling into a small place near a lake.

The limo pulls up near the building and parks. Roberto gets out and opens the door for me to get out, and helps me by holding out his hand. I step out and notice this is not a typical restaurant, if it is a restaurant at all.

"Roberto, where are we?"

"Ms. Rizzo, you are here for your dinner date."

UGH, why does everyone keep calling me Ms. Rizzo, and why

won't anyone tell me what is going on?

"Mr. Roberto, can you please tell me where I am, and who I am meeting. And can you please call me River?"

Roberto laughs. "Ms. Rizzo, I like the way that sounds. You have arrived for your dinner date, and all you have to do is walk inside the doors, and you will find out who asked you to come for dinner." He walks to the door of the building and opens it for me to go inside.

I stomp to the door and turn to Roberto. "Fine, Mr. Roberto, you wanna call me Ms. Rizzo, I will forever call you Mr. Roberto until you start calling me River. Which, by the way, is my name! Not Ms. Rizzo. And I guess I will walk myself in here and see who is in there, but I tell you what, it better not be Noah, or I am going to punch him for putting me through this!"

Roberto laughed and walked away. I walk into the building to find light classical music playing, a few tables, and no one else. Not even workers.

Great I'm going to get raped and murdered out here.

I turn to leave and get to the door.

"River," a voice behind me calls out, and it puts a smile on my face.

I turn around and run towards the voice.

"POPPY!!!" I screamed and then ran into him and embraced him in a hug. "I cannot believe I am seeing you. It's been eight years."

"I know my little pumpkin. I have missed you. Come sit. Let's eat." He pointed to a table and pulled out a chair for me to sit down.

I sit down all giddy to be having dinner with my Poppy. I notice off to the side that a waitress brings us sweet tea and salad. I start to eat a little bit and take a sip.

"Poppy, why are you in Vegas?"

"Oh, pumpkin, I had to come to take care of some business. How do you like Vegas so far?"

Well, all the bad news? What was I going to say?

"I'm not sure. Poppy, can I ask you something?"

"Pumpkin, what is wrong?" He puts down his fork and looks at me. His eyes pierce into mine as if to get the questions before I can ask him about them.

I am sitting there, lost for words, not even sure what to ask, or how to ask, or where to begin.

"Pumpkin, your Dad asked us to wait till you were old enough and done with high school before we told you anything. He would be very proud that you took your money and left your mom's house. There is a lot about your parents' past that you will learn about, but right now we need to focus on you getting stable and getting a job." He sighs as he knows this isn't the response I want. "Gramma also wanted me to tell you that you are safe. The best security in town will come in and protect you if you feel unsafe. All you have to do is ask, and there will be someone with you all the time." He takes my hand to reassure me. But it's not helping.

"Who did my Dad work for? My Mom asked me about Roman. Would that be the same as Roman?"

"Pumpkin, eat the chicken that the waitress brought you. Let's not waste our time on these questions, I want to show you something."

Waste our time? What about all the time I have wasted on my life to find out it is just a lie? I want to know what is going on, and if I have to do it on my own, I may just do that. I wonder how much Roberto knows? Everyone seems to know my grandparents. I wonder how much they know. I take a bite of my food and continue to ponder the thoughts in my mind.

I notice a guy out of the corner of my eye. Big, like the Rock big. Just as good-looking as him, too, standing by the exit on the other side of the room. He is talking quietly to himself. I try not to stare, as I am having dinner with my Poppy, and I want to spend time with him.

"Poppy, who knows about this place?" Just asking to reassure myself.

He laughs. "Well, it is on a public lake, but most people assume the building isn't used anymore. Why do you ask?"

Why is the Rock over there? I think to myself.

"He is here with me." He answers my question. Did I say that out loud?

"I'm sorry, Poppy. I thought I said that to myself."

He chuckles. "Finish eating." He says, pointing to my food.

I look down and see I have finished almost all of it, but I'm not hungry to eat anymore. I take a sip of tea and put down my fork. "I'm done, Poppy."

He wipes his hands and face off and takes a drink of tea. He gets up and pulls out my chair. "Come on, pumpkin, I have something for you."

I get up and follow him to another room that looks like an office. It has file cabinets along one wall and a desk in the center, along with a loveseat. Kind of reminded me of an office at a nightclub, like you see in the movies, and I laugh to myself when I think that.

"Sit, River," my grandpa says, as he pulls up the chair. He turns and goes and gets inside the desk.

I watch and wait patiently, with my nervousness making me a bit jumpy. He pulls out two boxes. One that is smaller in size, and another a little bit bigger. The bigger of the two had what looked like a funny lock on it.

"River, these are presents from your Dad." I can see he is going to cry, and I can't have that because I will end up crying too. He turns and grabs another box that is bigger than the big one on the table. He hands me the littlest box of them all. "Open it up."

I open the box, and instantly, the tears start to fall from my face. I found a necklace. It's a locket. Inside the locket is a pic of me and my Dad. The last one we had taken. It was my tenth birthday a week before he died. Or what I am finding out now, murdered. On the back it says: To my beautiful Swan Love Daddy. With the locket is a ring with a black diamond in the center and surrounded by pink diamonds. Black was Daddy's favorite color, and pink is mine. I can't stop crying.

Poppy got up and came around to hug me. He called to the bodyguard who looks like The Rock, whose name I have yet to get, or catch. He was told to take the other two boxes to my car.

"River dear, there is no rush for you to open the other two. But they are from your Dad as well." He takes the locket and puts it on me, so I am now wearing it. He removes the other one and puts it in the little box. I slide the ring onto the finger on my hand and move the red one to a different finger. Poppy then picks me up and gives me a big bear hug.

"How long are you in town for, Poppy?" I ask as I wipe away the tears.

"I have to head back tonight. I have been here for a few days, taking care of some business. I have to tie up some loose strings, then jump on the plane."

Loose strings?

I couldn't even get the question out when there was a loud noise out in the main area. We both take off running and find several guys with guns coming towards us. The Rock comes running towards Grandpa and me, and he scoops me up and runs back into the office, where Grandpa had already run.

He shut the door and locked it, and I could hear yelling that we were in the office. The men outside the office are yelling back and forth at each other. The office has bulletproof glass, so they can't shoot us in here.

"Poppy, what is going on? What is happening?" I can feel my body shaking, and I am freaking out with my nervousness right now.

"Listen, pumpkin, you need to stay calm and do exactly what we tell you to do. Breath River, Breath."

I shake my head yes.

"Good. Now take this gun."

I didn't agree to a gun, and I thought I was going to be safe.

"I don't know how to use it."

Poppy turned to the Rock and said something to him in Italian, and next thing I know, he gets up and moves a cabinet out of the way. I am even more confused and a door is exposed. He grabs me and puts me over his shoulder and takes off down a set of stairs. It is really dark now but the Rock keeps moving. Like he has been down this way before.

"Poppy?" I don't see him, and now I am scared.

"Mr. Rizzo will not be following us. I have to get you to safety, then I will go back in for him."

I start kicking and screaming, "You can't leave him in there."

"Ms. Rizzo, I have too!"

We make it to another door, and he swings it open, and just as he does, I feel something hit my head, or maybe I fall. Whatever it was, it made me black out.

12

Cain's Report

I hear a loud commotion around the back of the building, and the security guard who was with Mr. Rizzo starts yelling. I take off around the building and find Ms. Rizzo, I mean River, lying on the ground, and the security guard has a guy in a choke hold.

"He knocked her out. There is another guy who took off running that way, and there are still several inside with Mr. Rizzo."

I sent a text to Zeke: Compromised. Surveillance needs to be addressed; one got away, I'm going after, and we need someone inside to get Mr. Rizzo out. River is knocked out as well, we need to get her to the hotel.

I go over and pick up the angel from the ground and place her in the back of the limo, and instruct Roberto to get her out of here.

I went after the guy who took off running, but he went straight to the lake, and I lost his tracks in the lake.

"FUCK!!! HOW THE FUCK!!!" I turn and notice that Zeke is here and staring at me.

"Mr. Rizzo is out safe, and the goons with the guns are long gone, too. We got the one guy and are taking him back to base to question him."

"What about River? The innocent angel, so perfect, is going to be waking up soon, and we have to explain what happened to her." I am kind of yelling and kicking myself in the ass. One simple job, and I couldn't even do it.

Zeke chuckles, but I don't find any reason why he is or any of this to be a laughing matter. I stare at him like, what the hell, dude. He must have read my mind.

"You and Noah both. What is it about this girl?" He says, shaking his head.

Oh, he hasn't seen her yet, or he would be too. Noah, the lucky bastard, got to ride the bus home with her to make sure she was safe. What do I get to work at the stupid hotel? Why can't we just bring her up to speed and go on with our happy little lives?

"Mr. Rizzo is on the way to the hotel, his jet will leave after he makes sure she is OK. We will be meeting afterward, so let the rest of the team know. Jazmine is out on a mission and will not be there, so I will be filling in her spot."

I shake my head and send a mass text.

Text: Meeting on Mr. Rizzo's time. Will be at the jet for the meeting, so make yourself available. Zeke is in Jazz's spot for the meeting. Questions can be asked then. Mr. Rizzo is with the Swan.

I sure hope she is OK.

13

Hello Doctor

Oh, my head hurts. What the heck happened? I open my eyes and feel like I am in a strange place. I sat up real quick, rubbing my head and looking around. I'm in my room at the hotel. How did I get there? What do I remember? I got up and tiptoed out of the room, worried something bad had happened to me, or worse, to my Poppy.

I open the door and I can hear a voice. I listen. It's Poppy, he's OK, but who is he talking to? I stand still listening, but that is hard because my head hurts extremely badly right now.

"No, we are all OK. She was hit in the head, but we aren't sure why yet. We have to investigate a little bit more. Yes, when she wakes up and what not, I will be having a meeting before coming home. I may stay a few more days if we deem it necessary."

I heard Poppy talking, so I peeked into the dining room to find him on his phone. Was I the one who got hit in the head, because it sure does feel like it? And what meeting? Investigate who hit me, is that what he's talking about? He looked up and saw me peeking in the door and waved me in.

"Ah, River is awake now, darling. Say hi to Gramma. She wants to make sure you are OK." He hands me the phone.

"Hi, Gramma."

"Oh, River dear. Are you OK? How is your head? Do you remember anything that happened? Do you need Poppy to stay?"

I can't help but smile. My Mom would never even care to ask those questions. She probably would have blown up my cell phone, telling me to get home or else. I could have been dead in some alley if it had happened on her time, and she would never have known. Boy, I hate to think this, but I hate my Mom.

"Gramma, I am OK. My head hurts really, really bad, though. All I remember is being in the office and the Rock taking me through a secret door, and then my head hurting. I woke up here. If Poppy wants to stay, I will not complain." As I say that, I can see the smile on my face, and Poppy is looking at me.

"Well, I will call the doctor and have him come look in on you. Poppy will have to come home at least for a few days to take care of some business here. Then maybe both of us will come visit you."

I nodded but then remembered I was on the phone. I could hear Poppy chuckling as he saw me nod into the phone. "OK, but I don't think I need a doctor. I think some Motrin and water will make me feel better."

"Nonsense, dear, the doctor will come and take a look at you tonight. Take some Motrin and rest. Put Poppy back on. Love you."

"Love you too, Gramma." I turned and handed the phone to Poppy, who had water and Motrin sitting on the table next to him.

"River, do you need something to eat? Take these and go get

in comfy clothes to sleep in." Aw, Poppy worried about me. He talks on the phone super quickly. "Darling, I've got to go. Call the doctor. Love you too."

He hands me the water and the pills. I grab them from him and take them. "Poppy, I don't feel hungry right now. Thank you for staying with me. I am sorry I let this happen. Is the Rock OK?" Still not knowing the guy's name, I see Poppy smiling.

"The Rock feels bad that he let you get hit. He was able to capture one of the two guys who were waiting outside the building. Now, dear, go change out of those clothes, the doctor will be here shortly. I have to go for a meeting before heading back to Gramma. Will you be OK?"

Feeling sad, I knew he needed to go to work, so I pouted and shook my head yes.

"Come give Poppy a hug."

I run over, hug him, and he hugs me back. A great big bear hug. "Poppy, I love you. Be safe."

"Pumpkin, you be safe. I love you, too." He turns and leaves.

I sat down at the table and put my feet on another chair, debating on what I wanted to do. And this killer headache is not helping me at all. I start spinning and quickly learn that doesn't help at all, it makes it worse. Like when you spin till you're so dizzy and you end up puking. That was where I was at. I chuckle a little and get up and go to the backyard. Oh, the sun has set, and it's so bright. I want to go explore, but this headache won't let me. I can see all kinds of lights out past the wall that surrounds my backyard. Add to my must-do: go explore at night. Must see all the pretty lights.

I look down at the pool. And then notice the hot tub. Maybe a little bit of relaxing time in the hot tub would make me feel better. I turn and scan the area, no one can see in, and feeling too lazy to go to my room for a suit, I strip down right there and hop in.

Ah, this feels so good. I wish AnnaB were here. She would jump in with me. We do have a bit of a wild side to us. Part of the reason we are best friends.

Sitting there, I think back to this party that we went to. It was when we were like sophomores, and the guy she liked was a senior. He invited us to his party, the only underclassmen invited. We found our shortest skirts, which were plaid, like a schoolgirl, and matched. She wore a red low-cut shirt, and I wore a black one and had on thigh boots. We were the hottest girls there. Well, at least she was. The guys wouldn't stop staring at us. Of course, the senior girls didn't like that, so one walked up to AnnaB and was like; Only girls that skinny dip in the hot tub are allowed to stay. AnnaB asks the girl if that was so. And the girl was like, yeah. So only girls who skinny dip get to stay at the party, and the rest leave. It wasn't a huge party, but big enough to make a scene. What about the guys, is it the same for them she asks as she stared at the senior guy she had a crush on. He grinned and shook his head yes. AnnaB grabbed my hand and we walked to the backyard where we found a huge hot tub. It would fit thirty people in it. I was already shaking my head, but I knew what it meant to her. We undid our boots and started to undress with the senior girls watching with their jaws open. Both got in the tub completely nude. I, of course being the sassy ass I am asked who else was joining or who was leaving. About a dozen guys and a couple of girls jump in. The senior girl was completely stunned, and the guy asked her to leave. What a night. How could I be so stupid back then? It was a great night to remember, and new friendships were formed. And I didn't have to spend that time with my Mom. Yup, I am a bit of a rebel. Thinking about this made me laugh to myself.

I was so lost in my memory and forgot that I was expecting the doctor. When I heard a confused voice coming from behind me.

"Ms. Rizzo?"

I jumped and turned around. And was lost for words. I swear this town is nothing but hot gods, I mean guys. I was standing there, completely staring with my mouth wide open. I could feel my body temperature rising. This guy's blue eyes and dark hair that is long enough to flow into his face. Light stubble on his jawline. His bottom lip was so juicy and plump, I could kiss it. I could swear he was a model. And why was he in here? He was too young to be a doctor, looking not much over twenty or twenty-one. He was in shorts and a tank top as the temps were still warm outside, even in the night sky. He looked like he had just walked out of an Abercrombie and Fitch ad. I can see he was a little bit awkward as he was turning a pink shade.

He turned his head away from staring into my eyes, which made me snap back to reality and remember I was naked standing there. Now I was a dark shade of red. Like fire engine red.

"Um, it's River," I managed to say. "I am so sorry, I forgot you were coming, or more like I wasn't planning on you coming tonight. Wait, are you the doctor?"

I had turned around so my back was to him, but unsure of what I was going to do. I mean, I was standing there naked and with no towel.

He coughed, and I turned my head just to find that he had gone inside and grabbed me a robe. Oh, thank goodness.

"What was that, River? I missed what you had said." He grins at me, and I turn pink again.

Great River, what a great way to meet the doctor. And a hot one at that.

"I, um, was saying I didn't think you would come tonight. Are you a doctor? How did you get in here?"

"I knocked a couple of times, and when you didn't respond, I had housekeeping open the door. I was worried you had passed out or something. And yes, I am a doctor."

I take the robe and wrap it around me. The doctor opens the door and holds it open, waiting for me to go in. Which I do.

"I think I should throw on some clothes before you check on my body. Um, I mean, check my head out." Smooth, real smooth.

He chuckles and nods his head in approval, and I run to my room. Great, just great. I rush around and find a few things to put on. I don't want to keep him waiting too long.

I open my drawer and find really cute matching green boy short panties and bra, and toss those on. Next drawer I find P.J. shorts and a tank. I toss those on and calmly walk back out to the living space.

"OK, I am so sorry about that. Like I said, when my grand-mother said she was calling the doctor, I expected someone to come get me and take me to see the doctor tomorrow."

He smiled at me. "It's OK, River, I am Tatum. I am the doctor who handles issues here in Vegas for Mr. and Mrs. Rizzo if they need anything. So I guess I am now your doctor."

"What kind of issues do they have? How often do they come to Vegas?" Maybe I can get some answers to some of my questions from Doc Tatum. "How often do you see them?"

I think he sensed I was prying. "Come sit." He pats the spot next to him to have me come sit by him. "Let me take a look at you."

I walk over and sit down, completely aware that he is avoiding my questions. I also become very aware that my ass is hanging out of my shorts and I have to walk right past him. UGH, can this get any more awkward? I look at him and he is just being completely a gentleman, which makes me want to jump him even more. Goodness, he is so hot.

"How does your head feel?" As he looks at my eyes, a concerned face appears.

"It hurts. I have a killer headache, and I took some Motrin, and that didn't help any."

He excuses himself for a second and comes back with a bag a few minutes later. "I want you to take this." As he says that a knock at the door makes me jump.

I go to get it, and he makes it up before I do. It's Cain.

"Cain?" I ask.

"Um, hi Ms. Rizzo, I mean River. I brought the cot that was requested."

I stared at him, confused.

Tatum opens the door, and Cain comes in.

"River, I will be staying the night with you to make sure this head injury doesn't get worse and to keep an eye on you for the next twenty-four hours."

I was just standing there staring at both guys, but there was something odd about Cain, and I was trying to figure it out. When I remember he wore glasses earlier and looked more like Harry Potter, he is now missing his glasses, and looks more like Draco.

Two hot guys are standing here staring at me, and my mind wanders to what it would be like to kiss them and have their hands touching me. And even at this moment, it didn't bother me to have them both at the same time. River, I think you hit your head a little too hard. I can feel myself smirking while I was thinking these very improper thoughts, and forgetting they are both just standing there.

"River?"

I hear my name, but still lost in thought. I was imagining Tatum's lips on mine while Cain was behind me, caressing my back and nibbling on my ear.

"I think this is worse than I thought," Tatum says to Cain.

"River?"

"Oh, um, my bad, I was just thinking." I managed to say, unsure of who was talking to me.

They both chuckle, and I step aside. I begin to think maybe I might have been thinking that out loud. But too awkward to ask if I had, because if I hadn't, then they would want to know why. Boy, I am sure I hit my head a bit harder than I had thought.

Cain walks to my room, sets up the cot, and has a housekeeper bring blankets and stuff for Tatum.

While Cain was setting up the cot, Tatum handed me some pills.

"What are these?" I was unsure if I should take them.

"Magical pain pills," he says, laughing.

Oh, Lord, please help me. I take them.

"Good night, Ms. Rizzo, I mean, River." Cain says, "I will see myself out." And he leaves before I can even say goodnight.

I grab my phone just as Tatum tells me I need to lie down. So I head to my bed and lie down, and look at my messages.

Text: OMG, girl, I am jealous. Send more pics. I already booked my flight for Christmas. Love you, girl. <3 AnnaB

Text Back: I secretly took this pic for you. There are only hot gods out here. I mean, guys. This, my friend, is my doctor, and he is staying the night. Three hot guys I have met, if you don't count the *guy I call the Rock. 'Cause girl, he looks like The Rock. We are in for some fun in December. Miss you, girl. <3 River*

Attached was a picture of Tatum.

Text: River, Mom is at rehab again. I got her when she wasn't high, and she was yelling about that Roman guy you mentioned. She said she was going to die, so I took her to the mental hospital, and they are detoxing her. Will update you later on that. Now, about that boy. Any words? I mean, what kind of idiot is he?

That made me giggle a little bit inside. Grandma always knows how to make me laugh. I turn and see Tatum staring at me from the chair in my room.

"What?" I ask him.

"Your giggle is so cute; it makes me smile."

Is he flirting, or am I high?

"Sorry, a message from my Grandma made me giggle." Play it safe.

He doesn't say anything but just keeps staring at me.

I turn back to my phone and see a message from Gramma.

Text: The Doctor will be there in about thirty minutes. Love you, darling.

I text Gramma back: TOOOOOO LATE, Gramma, and why didn't you tell me he was hot? And he saw me naked already because I didn't see your message.

Yup, I am high from the pill. I burst out in laughter from my message, and I know Gramma is going to freak out.

Tatum is chuckling now. I turn and look at him. "What is so funny?"

"I am not sure, why don't you tell me?" He says, smiling at me.

"Well, my Gramma sent me a message to tell me you were coming, but I just got it. I told her she was too late and asked why she didn't tell me you were hot, and that you already saw me naked. Then I started to laugh because she is going to freak out." Can I say foot in mouth right now? "Are these truth pills or something?"

He laughs even harder. "How does your head feel?"

I thought about it. "Not as bad as earlier."

"Good, so they are working. Now, you think I am hot, huh?" he says, smirking at me.

"Duh!" damn it River. "I am feeling tired, but I want to cuddle." Yup, you are one sly girl, aren't you?

Tatum looks at me. "I am not going to take advantage of you while you are on those pain meds, and I will not allow you to try and take advantage of me. But if you want me to lie next to you so you can sleep, I will be more than willing to."

"Please?" I look at him with sad eyes, I wanted to have his arms around me just so I can feel safe. Because safe wasn't what I was feeling. I even bat my eyelashes at him.

He lay down next to me, and I grabbed his arm and wrapped it around me and cuddled my back up against his chest. He chuckled a little, and I let out a sigh of relief.

14

Kiss

I roll over in the middle of the night, and my arm hits someone, or something. My head is pounding again, too. I looked at what was next to me, and to my surprise, it was the hot doctor. How the heck did he get in bed with me? I lifted my blankets and made sure I was still in clothes. Not that I would be disappointed if I hadn't been, but I would like to remember doing something fun with him. Look at him, you would too. He must have felt me moving.

"How is your head?" he calmly asks me. Barely opening his eyes. At least he knew where he was and who was next to him.

"It hurts again." Well, it is the truth, but really, I didn't want him to leave.

He rolled over and grabbed me some more medicine, and I took them. "What are these magical pills?" Not caring but wanting to make some small talk.

"Just some pain meds. Do you want me to move to the cot now?" He grabs his little light thing and starts to look into my eyes.

"No!" I said probably a little too fast.

He laughs. "OK, then. So what made you come to this crazy town?"

I was feeling a little bit still loopy from the meds from before when I replied to him. "My Mom is a loser, and never loved me. I needed to free myself from the chains she was locking me down with. I went to the bus station, and that was when Vegas chose me." Wow, did I just say that about my Mom? Now I am embarrassed. I wasn't embarrassed as to the fact that I was here, but that I just opened up kind of about my Mom. Was I ready to share this with the hot doc?

He sat up and took off his shirt. I started to drool, I am sure of it. His body was defined, nice lickable abs. Is lickable even a word? I mean, I want to lick them. I want to do more than just lick them. He lay back down and brought me closer to him, putting his arm under my head.

"My Mom was the same way. She was never even around. I think she only kept me around because of the child support money she got from my Dad. The day I graduated from high school, I found a couple of suitcases outside on the porch, and the door lock had been changed."

I wanted to cry. He had it almost worse than I. At least my Mom didn't kick me out. But whatever I wish, she had it would make things easier. I found myself resting my head on his shoulder. And liking it. I have never felt this close to anyone, let alone a guy I have only known for I don't know, a few hours. I wasn't sure if it was the magical pills he had given me or if I was feeling close to him.

He looked down at me. I could feel his eyes on my head, and I wanted to look up and kiss him, but I was so uncertain of how he would feel about it. I could stay like this forever.

"I am sorry your Mom did that to you. My Mom didn't kick

me out, but I couldn't stay there anymore. I always had to pick up the pieces and take care of her. I really need to go. And there was no looking back."

He pulled me up closer to his face, and his beautiful eyes were piercing into mine. I could feel the hurt from his past, and I am sure he could feel it in mine. His lips were calling to me, and I knew he was thinking about kissing me as he stared at my lips. I licked them as I wanted him to kiss them, and bit the side of the bottom lip.

"How can you do this to me?"

Huh, do what? Now I am lost at what I was doing. "Do what to you?"

"Look at me like that. I am having a hard time controlling myself right now."

"Ever think I might not want you to control yourself?" Doh, River, what the heck. Must be the pills, I swear they are truth pills.

He smirked at me. I know he could see that my body was heating up from what I had just said. I leaned over and kissed him. If he wasn't going to make a move, well, I will then. I wanted to taste his lips. I needed to taste those lips. I need to taste him. I needed to feel him.

At first, I lightly pushed my lips to his, waiting to see how he would react. Waiting to see if he pulled away, or if he would kiss me back. He didn't pull back, so I leaned in a little harder, and I could feel he was kissing back. I reach up to his messy hair and run my fingers through it as I lightly run my tongue along his bottom lip. I find his tongue running along my top lip, and I open my mouth to invite it in. I feel his tongue and swirl it around his tongue, and he tries to explore my mouth with his tongue, and I do the same with his. Our tongues bouncing off each other's tongues and exploring inside each other's mouths. I would even run my tongue on his lips.

Oh. My. God. He can kiss, and his lips are just as tasty as they look. I find that I start to bite lightly on his bottom lip, pulling it towards me, and he lets out a groan. Mm, he likes that, and I start kissing again, and biting his lip. I can feel him getting excited as his hands run up my back. His fingers run into my hair, pulling me harder into him. I start to kiss down his jawline to his ear, where I start to nibble on his lobe. He moans even louder. And I find that he is nibbling on my ear. I let out a moan, and it excites me. I pull him closer into my body, not that he can get any closer.

Next thing I know, he has rolled me over and is now on top of me, kissing me way more passionately. I find my hands running down his back. His skin is so smooth and soft. I find that they are running down to his butt and I grab it. Nice, I can feel myself smiling. Which makes him kiss me harder. I run my nails back up his back, and I can feel him tense up on top of me.

He starts kissing down my jawline, and down my neck, and up to my ear, where he nibbles a little more, and it makes me moan even louder. I pull him harder into my body. With my nails starting to dig into his back a little. Wanting more. I start to kiss his ear, sucking a little on his lobe and nibbling a little bit too. Taking it lightly in my teeth and pulling it a little bit. I can tell he likes that, and likes it a lot. I decided to bite, well, not hard, on his neck. And the moans get even louder and heavier than before, so I continue down his chest. He stops kissing me and lays his head on my shoulder as he moans.

He feels down my sides with his hands till he gets to my waist. He grabs the bottom of my shirt and lifts it over my head. Now

I am lying here in my bra, and he kisses down my neck and nibbles on it as well. This makes me very moist and wanting to flip him over and jump him. I want to ride the hell out of him. Like seriously, how can I even let him do that without jumping him? He kisses and licks his way on the top of my boobs that are popping out of the top of my bra. His head is down in my breast, and I can't even kiss him. I continue to run my fingers down his neck very lightly, and I can feel the shivers they are sending up his spine. He continues to kiss down to my belly button. I let out a loud moan. And he kisses back up to my mouth. My God, what is he doing to me? My head is spinning, and I want this to last forever. I go back to nibbling on his ear and his neck and biting his chest. I love the way he wiggles and the way his body shakes on top of me. I can feel that someone else wants to play rubbing on me, causing me to moan out with excitement. He kisses me hard and brings my hands above my head as he kisses, making me even hotter for him.

Then he stops kissing me and looks into my eyes. He is just looking at me. Deep into my eyes, looking at me.

"Tatum? What's wrong?"

He rolls off me. And I can say I am disappointed. No, very disappointed. He wraps me up and kisses my head, and keeps me close to him.

"Babe, I can't."

He can't what? Perform? Um, yeah, he can, I felt it. And let me just say. I wanted it. Just thinking about it makes me blush.

"You can't, what? Because I am sure you wanted to." Boy, I am still blaming it on the pills.

He laughs. Great, he laughs at me as if that is supposed to make it better. He can't do it with me, and now he laughs at me. I must be some sort of freak.

I let out a breath because of the frustration. And that makes Tatum laugh even more.

"It's not that, I want to. Boy, do I want to. I just don't want to do it like this. I want you to remember it. And for it to be special. Or at least more special. And I want to get to know you better." He says to me, and I can tell he means it. "Plus, we both agreed we wouldn't. Not tonight anyway."

I sigh, but it makes a lot of sense. "Promise me you will take the time to get to know me then." Boy, do they make these pills in a non-drowsy form? They make me more straightforward than I have ever been.

He smiled. "Yes, yes, I promise. How about I spend the day with you tomorrow?"

A whole day with a hot doctor? Who am I to say no? "Doctor knows best," I say with a smirk.

"That he does." He leans over and kisses the top of my head, and wraps his arms around me to cuddle up next to me.

At this moment, I was finally feeling like I was someone. And that I belong somewhere. For this moment, I felt as if my life was starting to be what I had hoped it would be. And boy, would Grandma be happy to hear about my doctor friend. Maybe I should take a pic cause she won't believe it if she doesn't see it. Not tonight, I am too tired. Not to mention, I have no shirt on. She wouldn't like that. Or maybe she would.

Tatum picks up my hand and wraps his in mine and kisses it.

"Good night, Babe."

Aw, he called me babe for the second time. Was he giving me a nickname? I would call him abs. Oh, I am messed up once again. My brain won't let me think straight.

"Good night, Doc." I giggle as I say it. I can't call him abs. So doc it is.

Next thing I know, my eyelids are getting heavy and I am starting to fall asleep. I am still wondering if it was something I did that made him stop. He was ready, boy was he ready. I was ready. But he stopped. And I........

15

Poppy's Report

"Hello," I say as I answer the phone.

"Tatum says it is worse than we first thought. I am taking a cot to her room. He needs to stay for the next twenty-four to thirty-six hours just to make sure. If there is no improvement, we will take her to the office for some CT scans. He doesn't seem to think it will come to that."

It was Cain who was giving me an update on my pumpkin. I wasn't able to stay. I had to get home as there was another emergency we had to take care of before I could come back and spend a few days with her.

Boy, my little pumpkin sure has grown up. She is a beautiful lady, and I can tell the boys seem to have taken a liking to her. It's no wonder she is all they talk about. But they better not hurt a hair on her head or else. I chuckle as I say that because I know better. They won't hurt her; it will end up being her that hurts them. A girl after my own heart. I just hope she doesn't have to get caught up in this mess.

"Cain, keep me posted. Did we get anywhere with the guy we caught?"

"Nope, Sir, I am sorry. We will keep trying."

I hang up, knowing this guy will either let us know if it's Roman that sent him, or someone else we need to worry about.

I know we need to tighten up security until we know for sure.

16

Punch

As I yawn and stretch, I start to open my eyes. Boy, I slept well. What do I smell? I completely open my eyes and yawn again. It smells good. I roll over and find that Tatum is no longer in bed with me. Hmm, well, I must have dreamed all of that last night. Those pills did me in. I roll out of bed.

I walk out into the living room, still in search of the smell. Nothing. Disappointment fills my body. I turn and go to the makeshift dining room and find the smell is stronger. Smells like bacon. Yummy. I continue to walk into the kitchen, beginning to wonder if Tatum is in there cooking. I sure hope so, a hot guy that can cook. I would then say I have died and gone to heaven.

As quietly as I can, tiptoe to open the door on the other side of the dining room and slowly open it. I stopped dead in my tracks. It's not Tatum I see in there. My mouth drops open, I bet it hit the floor.

"Well, good morning. Aren't you just peachy in the morning?"

Still in shock, I manage to compose some words. "What are

you doing?"

Cain laughs at me. "What does it look like I am doing? Making you breakfast."

"Why are you here, and cooking me breakfast?" Why is the front counter manager cooking me breakfast? I mean, I didn't mind, but this seems a bit odd to me.

"Um, I just told you. I am making breakfast. Now go and put on some clothes." He points at my chest.

I look down. I stare at my chest. Shit, I have no shirt on, just a bra. Wow, what a great impression I am leaving on everyone. Where did my shirt go?

Oh....

Last night wasn't just a dream.

I look up and see that Cain is still smiling at me, and I get the urge to kiss him. But after last night, I got to keep my hormones in check.

"Must have been some night last night," Cain says to me, laughing. "You should see your face right now, how confused it is."

Still just staring at him, lost for words, I am frozen in my place. How do I even begin to explain this? Do I even need to explain this to him? I mean, he only works the counter.

"If I must say, it was, um, yeah, never mind. It's not like anything happened." I find I had to say that, but unsure why I felt the need to say it. I turned and walked out.

I can hear him laugh still in the kitchen. That makes me stomp back to my room. I look for some clothes to put on. I grab a skirt and top and head to the bathroom, figuring I could take a quick shower; I turn on some music from my iPhone dock that is wired to the bathroom.

I go and enter the bathroom, singing to the music that is

playing, lost in my thoughts. I throw my clothes on the floor. "But I'll be your daydream, I'll wear your favorite things, we could be beautiful, get drunk on the good life, I'll take you to paradise, say you'll never let me go." Singing this while I step into the huge shower and turn on and let out a scream.

I was totally in shock, and I heard someone come running into the bathroom.

"River, are you OK?" I can hear Cain's voice standing in the bathroom, and he moves closer to the shower stall and opens it. His cheeks turn red, then he begins to laugh. "Um, I am very sorry, I thought you were hurt. But it's nothing the doctor can't take care of."

That remark makes Tatum laugh. Who was standing in the shower with me.

I throw my hands up. Then remember, now I am standing there completely naked. Cain must have seen me blushing, and he laughs, turns, and goes to leave. "By the way, River, you have nothing to be ashamed of." Quickly turning and smiling at me, and winking before he closes the door.

Now, is it awkward that Cain just said that, looked at me naked, then left me in the shower with Tatum? Still in shock that neither one of them seemed to mind that the other one saw me naked. But then again, it's not like I was either one of their girlfriends. As far as I know, they could have girlfriends. Why didn't this dawn on me last night?

Still standing there, dazed. Lost at what I should say, I mean, for Pete's sake, I am standing in the shower naked with a hot guy. And there goes my eyes down his body. Hot Damn, it's getting hot in here. Those abs are going into that V, and hello. Um, yeah, that is nice. River, pull your eyes off him. I eye him back up the body and notice he is standing there grinning. Not that huge teeth showing grin, just the corner of his lips turned up just enough to know I got caught. But Damn, I want to get caught with my hand in the cookie jar, if the cookie jar is him.

"Well," Tatum says to me, still standing there.

I blush, and my body tingles. "Well, this is a bit awkward. In a nice kind of way."

This makes him chuckle. "I was actually about to get out. I'll see you at breakfast." He goes to leave, and I move so he can get out. He walks towards me.

He grabs me, picks me right up off the floor, and wraps my legs around him to help keep my balance. He leans me against the wall of the shower. I wrap my arms around his back and run my hands up to his wet hair. He leans into me and kisses me. He runs his tongue along my bottom lip, waiting for me to let him in. I grab hold of his tongue in my teeth, just barely, and I can feel him moan on my lips. I let go and grabbed his lip. The moan that escapes makes me a bit moist, who am I kidding, it makes me wet. I want to feel him inside of me.

He stops kissing me, again, even when I could feel him wanting to enter me. Knowing he wants to do it, but he doesn't. WHY, what is wrong with me? Leaning down, he is kissing me again.

"Babe, shower, I will be waiting for you at breakfast."

Boy, he has much more restraint than I do. I stand there watching him dry off and wrap a towel around himself. He, my friend, was still excited. And the tent was proof of it. He walked out in just his towel, leaving me in the shower, overly excited as well.

I turn the water on cold for a few minutes to bring down my heated body temperature. I stand under it for what must have been a longer time than just a couple of minutes because I start to shiver, and Tatum and Cain both come back in to check on me.

"Are you OK?" Cain asks me, and Tatum is staring at me seeing I am shivering.

He comes over and instructs Cain to grab some towels. He turns the water on to help warm me up.

"Babe, what were you doing taking a cold shower?"

That makes me laugh, and I turn to him and just stare at him.

He begins to blush a little bit.

"Hey, want to fill me in?" Oh, poor Cain.

"It's nothing," both Tatum and I say at the same time. Which makes us laugh.

Cain shakes his head, "Sure, it was nothing. We have a frozen River, and a blushing Tatum, and poor me sitting here trying to pretend I am stupid." He hands the towels to Tatum and goes out of the bathroom.

Tatum wraps me up with the warm towels and carries me to my bed, where I find Cain going through my dresser, finding clothes. Holding up some panties, "What about these?".

"Dude, it doesn't matter, just give me some clothes," Tatum yells at him as he is rubbing my body because I am still shivering.

It was kind of fun having two guys dress me. I think I may have to do this again. I didn't even have to lift a leg. Ha-ha, they did it for me. I didn't even mind that I was once again exposed for the world to see, because it wasn't as bad. I had a towel on, and they lifted my panties up, but kept my towel down, which made me chuckle.

"I think she did this on purpose." Cain finally said to break the silence.

"I don't think so," Tatum said, shaking his head.

"Maybe, I did. Maybe I wanted to be dressed by two hot gods." Oh. My. God. Did I just say that? Tell me, I just thought that to myself, and not out loud. And why can't I say guys?

I could tell by the way the guys were looking at me that I said it out loud. I bring my hand to my face and *Face-palm.*

They both stare at me, then they exchange looks, then laugh.

They didn't mention it while we all walked to the living room, where they had the TV on and food on plates already. I sat on the couch, and both guys decided to sit next to me. Oh, Lord, it is going to be a long day today, I can see it.

I began to eat my bacon and watch the news on the TV, when I decided I didn't want to watch the news anymore, and grabbed the remote. I switch the channels till I find something that I want to watch. Yup you guessed it, Cruel Intentions. Bahaha I start laughing and the gods, I mean guys look at me. Then at each other.

"So you think we are gods, huh?" Cain asks, lighting up the mood, so to speak.

"I did not say gods, I said guys." Yup, this is my story, and I will stick to it. I turn to him and stick my tongue out.

Just then, Tatum gets a page. "Babe, I will be right back. I have to run to the office for about an hour, will you be OK with Cain?"

"Um, I'm not sure about him," I smirk at him.

Tatum laughs and gets up. I follow him to the door, and he turns and kisses me deeply and passionately. "I will be right back, I promise." He turns and he leaves.

I turn around and see Cain standing there. Um, that is kind of creepy.

"So what is the deal with you and the doc?"

Is he prying? "What do you mean?"

He shakes his head, walks over to me, grabs my hand, and walks me back to the living room. He sits down and pulls me onto his lap. OK, isn't this a bit weird? I mean, he just saw me kissing Tatum, and now he has me on his lap?

"How do you know Tatum?" I try to turn to see him, and he only moves me a little bit, but still has me on his lap.

"We have been friends for a long time. Like, since we were little."

"Does he have a girlfriend? Do you have a girlfriend?" I can't leave him out, I can't make him feel bad, I asked.

He sits there like he is lost in thought or looking for the right response. Either one of them has a girlfriend. Or both.

He leans in real close to my ear and whispers, "No, not yet." His breath on my ear makes me tingle. But I just kissed Tatum, and it would be weird if I kissed Cain. Wouldn't it? I can feel the tension with us and with him as he is still lingering at my ear with his light breath on it.

His phone rings. Saved by the bell. I get up and take this time to go to my room and get my phone.

Text back from AnnaB: Um, girl, tell me you are at least having fun with that guy. Doctor huh? OK, maybe I will skip MSU and come now. I mean, three hot gods? You may need a hand. Or two. Oh, the dirty thoughts. I wanna see more. <3

I sneak out and snap a pic of Cain and attach it to a text.

Text back: Meet Cain. I am not sure what his role is as he was cooking me breakfast, found me naked in the shower, twice, and was just now, I think, trying to kiss my ear. But I made out with the doctor. And I could feel he wanted me. And the tent said so too. ;-) please help!!!

Text to Grandma: What about a hot doctor instead? Let me know about Mom. Love you, Grandma. I was sort of sick. I hit my head.

Text from Gramma: Well, dear, that puts you in a bit of an awkward situation. :D I hope you had fun. Love you. And BTW the doctor IS hot.

My eyes popped out of my head when I read that message from my Gramma. I guess my Gramma is only human, right?

A ping on my phone made me jump.

AnnaB: Ummm, dumb ass, you're young and not married, who says you have to pick one hot god. I mean, if you need some help, I can always come there and help you out. Take a few off your plate. But if it were me, well, we all know how crazy I am. I would be fucking them all. Pardon my French. But you know it's true. Quit worrying that you will turn out to be like your Mom and all her boyfriends. You're not her. You are you. And to have a few FB's never hurt anyone. Just don't go all crazy and sleep with all of Vegas. Live a little, that's why you're there, right?

Very true, AnnaB, very true. I was smiling at my phone when Cain walked into my room.

"What are you smiling at?" he asks me as he walks in.

Does he know how to knock? I don't remember saying Come in.

"Nothing." I set my phone down and got up. "Don't you know how to knock? Don't remember seeing a sign saying "Cain's room."

Cain walks over to me, "Remind me to change that." He grabs my phone and starts going through it.

OH HELL NO HE DIDN'T!

"What the hell are you doing?" I scream at him and run after him.

He holds it high above his head where I can't reach it. And starts scrolling through my messages. OK, that's it. I throw a punch right in his gut, and he bends over and drops my phone.

"Um, what is going on here?" I hear Tatum saying behind me. a

I rush over to my phone and pick it up. "Nothing. Someone decided he needed to let me practice how to punch." I turn to Cain with a shit grin on my face.

Tatum starts laughing.

Cain still bent over holding his gut, "Did you know she took a pic of you last night? Not to mention one of me today?"

My eyes open wide. My jaw drops. He read my messages, too, the bastard. I walk over and punch him in the gut again. Exs

17

Jazmine's Report

Oh, boy, we are in trouble with this girl. These stupid boys.

"We need to discuss this," I turn and tell Mykayla (Aka KK or Macky)

Mykayla looks at me, rolling her eyes.

"Boys will be boys, but are they willing to play with their emotions with this girl? I mean, three of them are already falling for her. What will it do to this team? I thought we said to date outside the circle. I mean, I wanted to be with Noah, and you suggested that I back off."

Mykayla was right, but River isn't part of the circle. On top of it, I didn't want her to date within the circle because she is too crazy for the boys. I chuckle to myself thinking about it. "River is the target of Mykayla, not the circle." I knew she probably would end up in the circle, but if the boys are all ogling her, would it even work? "Besides, you have that great guy, Rafael. He is way hotter than Noah, or any of the guys."

"So, what do you suggest? They all date her?" She says, laughing. But you know what, that sounded like a good thing. I mean, what better way to find out who she is than for them to "date" her and get her to open up. Maybe we can find out who she is after her that way. That loser of a mother of hers.

I turn back on the camera in time to see River punch Cain in the gut, for a second time. I had been watching the interactions with her and the boys all day, and Cain and Tatum don't seem to be bothered. But she is hesitant about the idea. She even texted her friend about it.

Note to self: find out what I can about this AnnaB girl.

I notice Mykayla is staring at me.

We need a meeting. We need to figure out who is after Rosalie Hammond and River. I sent out a text.

Text to Circle: We need a meeting. When Sleeping Beauty is better and can be alone for a few hours, we need to meet. The meeting will be at my place. Tatum, let us know when it will be clear to go.

Now my only worry is what happens if they all fall for her, could this ruin the circle? Could this ruin the guys?

18

Player's Lounge

Both the guy's phones ping at the same time. I look at them and start laughing. Which lightens the tension in the room?

Tatum walked over to me and picked me up, and put me on the couch. "First, I need to check out the newest victim of abuse. Then I will be back to give you a look over."

He walks over to Cain and double-checks that he is OK. Now come on, according to Noah, I hit like a girl, so it shouldn't hurt. Noah, how I missed the fun we had on the bus. I was so stupid; I should have gotten his number. Not that Cain and Tatum weren't good eye candy. He just made this trip here fun. I would like to go out sometime with him.

Tatum walking back to me snapped me out of my memories.

"Hey, Cain, you know, in the last few days, you're not the only guy I have hit. And the other guy told me I hit like a girl. Would you agree?"

This seemed to pique his interest. He smirks at me, "You hit someone else? When? And I would have to agree, you do hit like a girl."

Oh, the nerve of him. I picked up the pillow next to me since

Tatum was looking at me, so I couldn't get up and go punch the fool again. I whipped the pillow at his head, and the corner of it hit him in the eye. I busted out laughing.

"Ouch, my eye. You took out my eye. I think I'm blind now."

This made me laugh even harder. "Now, who's the girl?"

This made Tatum laugh, too. "She does have a point, dude, you're not blind. But you sure are crying like a little girl. At least River didn't cry when she got knocked out."

"Not fair. She was knocked out, no time to cry." He pleaded in his defense.

"So, babe, I think you are looking better. I think I will take off. I have some work to do, and so does Cain. But if you would like, I can stop back before you go to bed, or Cain can."

"Yeah, that's fine. I have a few things I want to do. Is it safe to explore some? I want to see Vegas. Not be in a room the whole time, or I just might have to move to another city."

"How about a deal? Take it easy today and explore inside the hotel, play some slots, and eat some dinner in the Player's Lounge. I will come back around tonight."

OK, time to be a little bold, like AnnaB told me. "So, do I get phone numbers in case I need something?" Bingo, I get bonus points. Thank you for making me have a backbone. I smile inside, not wanting to have the guys question me about my smirk.

They both look at each other and shrug. "May I have your phone? Without being hit this time." Cain politely asked. I hand it over so he can program his number. "I am going to text myself so I have your number too, I mean, if that is OK with you."

Um, hello, yeah, it's OK, why wouldn't it be OK? You can text me whenever you want. I nod at him, too worried I might have a slip of the tongue again to talk. He hands the phone to Tatum, who looks at the phone shaking his head laughing.

"Dude? Hottest God Ever? You put that in there?" Tatum looks at Cain, who is now smirking.

"Don't be jealous that I'm the hottest god and you're not."

"You only wish."

Boy, they are both gods.

OK, why are they both looking at me? Oh, Lord, my face is heating up. I have a feeling I said that out loud. Why does this keep happening to me?

"Why are you both staring at me?"

"We are both gods, huh?" Tatum finally broke the ice.

Yup, I sure did say that out loud. And I am sure I am beet red.

They laugh and hand me back my phone. Tatum says, "Cain is now in there as Cain. I am here as Doc. Is that OK?"

Still too embarrassed by the fact I stated out loud that I just nod yes.

Cain walks over and picks me up, and hugs me, a big bear hug. I find it to be very comforting. And he kisses the top of my head. Um, this is weird. But Tatum didn't say anything. He sets me on the floor. And walks to the entrance of the living room, waiting for Tatum.

Tatum walks over and picks me up with his hands on my ass. I wrap my legs around naturally. He leans into my lips and kisses me. I bite his lip, and he moans. I rub my tongue along my lip.

"Do you two need privacy? I mean, we have stuff to do. No time for that now." Cain says, breaking the mood. But not in a jealous tone, in a playful tone. "I mean, if you two need a room, I can guide you in that direction."

Which makes both of us laugh. Tatum leans in and pecks me

on the lips, "I will come by later. Text me if you want to talk or whatever." Then sets me down.

"OK, man, that was just wrong," Tatum says to Cain as they start to walk out.

"Well, it's not fair you kissing her like that when I want to kiss her like that."

Did I just hear that right? Did Cain just tell Tatum he wanted to kiss me like he was kissing me? I walked to the door, and they just went out and cracked it because I was worried that there was going to be a fight. But there wasn't a fight. I think I hear Tatum say he didn't care if Cain kissed me like that. But I am not sure.

Oh, girl, you've gone crazy. Guys don't like things like that. I close the door and head to my room. I look at the boxes my Dad gave me. The latter of the two had a special lock on it. It was weirdly shaped. No, a normal key would fit inside it. How the hell do I open this? Messing around the box for a while and still no luck, and I sat it down. I go and pick up the big box and set it on the floor next to the bed. I opened it up. Inside it are a bunch of files. Why would my Dad give me a box of files? I pull out the file on top and open it. I nearly dropped the whole file on the ground.

I am staring at the picture on top of the file. It is a picture of a very young woman who looks much like me. She looks happy and not all doped up on drugs. She is smiling and sitting on a bench in the park with a couple of girls. Girls who look like a few of Mom's old friends. But they are much younger, too. She looks like she is about fifteen or sixteen in the picture. She looks like the light of the moon. Such a beautiful smile on her face and is so full of life. Where is that girl now? I mean, I know it's my Mom, but it's not my Mom, that is not the woman I know.

I flip over to the next picture of my Mom and some man I have never met. She was on him, kissing him. In the next picture, I see my Mom snorting lines off a guy's chest. She was still so young and must have been about sixteen. There were pictures of my Mom dealing. Pics of my Mom I didn't want to see. I am assuming the guy in these pics is that guy, Roman. I looked through pics. I saw pics of my Dad going to where my Mom was. The night and shining armor are coming in. As I was putting pictures together and laying them out. I see a picture of my Dad and Mom together, and it makes me remember the time when I was about five. My Mom and Dad took me to the zoo. My Mom smiled at my Dad and me the same way he is in this picture. I have no idea why my Mom and Dad never got married. They were so happy and so in love. I wish I had a pic of that night now, of us at the zoo together.

A few hours have passed and I have only seen pics up to the point where my Mom and Dad got together, but not together, cause my Mom went back to that Roman (I think it's Roman) right after she left my Dad's apartment.

A ping on my phone brings me back to life. I look down at the message.

Text from Superman: Who is Superman?

Message: Hello beautiful, sorry I haven't sent you a text. But since the bus ride things have been, well, not what I was hoping. I hope you're getting settled in. I was wondering if you wanted to meet in the Player's Lounge for a late dinner or a few drinks. I mean, I forgot your eighteen, coffee?

Noah! Superman is Noah! And how I had been worried he didn't like me.

Text back: How did you get my number? And what time?

I had barely hit send on the message when I got a message back.

Text from Noah: On the bus, and how about around 8:45?

I look at the time, it's 7:30 now.

Text back: Sure, see you then. <3

I sent Tatum a message telling him I was meeting a friend at 8:45 for dinner, and he replied saying he would come over later if I wanted him to. I told him I would let him know. And he said OK, and to have fun.

I went to the closet to get dressed. I found a black dress, just above the knees, with a wrap on one shoulder, and it was puffy. Put that on and pulled my hair up in a bun, and I put on some silver heels. I didn't want to be in all black. I put on the locket that Daddy had given me and the ring as well. I made my way down to the Player's Lounge.

"May I help you?" said the lady at the door.

"Hi, I am River Hammond. Charlie Rizzo is my grandmother. I am meeting a gentleman named Noah here tonight." I look at the time and see that it is 8:15. "I am a little early, he will be coming shortly."

"Yes, Ms. Rizzo, welcome to the Player's Lounge. Have a seat anywhere." She opened the door and let me in. Did she just call me Ms. Rizzo, too?

I walk in and find that it is a little bit crowded. I make my way to a quiet corner and sit down, and send a text to Noah telling him I'm here already.

"Well, aren't you beautiful? And easy on the eyes."

I hear an unfamiliar voice. And look up. A not-too-shabby younger guy was standing there.

"Is that supposed to impress me? I have heard better pickup lines from a five-year-old." I replied to him.

He chuckles and reaches his hand out to me. He wanted to shake my hand, but I just stared at it. I wasn't about to shake his hand. I didn't even want him over here. "Well, I can see it will take a lot more than some silly line with you. My name is Jackson. Do you mind if I sit?" As he takes a seat on the chair next to the couch I am sitting on. He doesn't even wait for me to tell him no. Please help me, I don't want him sitting here.

"What brings a beautiful girl like you to a lounge full of guys?" He looks at me and waves his hand around the room.

"I am meeting my boyfriend here." I didn't know what else to say. I want him to leave and leave me alone. "So, I guess you should maybe leave?"

"Ah, a boyfriend. Yeah, well, if that is the case, I could at least buy you a drink and keep you company till he gets here. Maybe I can convince you to give me your number anyway."

Yeah, right, creepy guy is not going to get my number, but sure I could use a drink. "I think I will pass on the drink."

"Oh, come on, let me get a drink. If your boyfriend hasn't shown up by then, I will leave you be. Just one drink won't hurt."

Well, that didn't seem to be unreasonable, did it? "I will take bottled water."

He laughs and gets up, and walks to the bar. I look around the bar and see that the club is full of many guys. Some old, some young, some cute, and then not so cute. Along with very few, very attractive women. I begin to wonder if they are called girls or gold diggers.

Jackson walks back over with a drink, but it's not water. "Um, I asked for water." I hand back the drink.

He laughs, "They don't typically serve water in this bar, so I ordered you a Sex on the Beach."

I have had drinks before, so it wasn't like one drink would do anything to me. So I took a drink of it.

I made small talk with this guy, but he wasn't very interesting. I look at my phone. Boy, what time does it say I can't even read it?

"Miss, are you OK?" Jackson said to me.

"I don't know. I feel like I am drunk. I think I need to go to my room."

I try to read the time again, and it's just blurry. I feel like I am going to be sick. I stand up, and the room starts to spin. I see faces become blurry and are starting to look all deformed. I take a step and almost fall. My eyes roll to the back of my head, and I feel myself falling, but I cannot do anything but fall. I can hear movement, and someone picks me up. But I have no idea who. I can feel myself being carried and hear muffled voices. Next thing I know, I feel myself being thrown onto something, and more muffling voices.

19

Escape

Ouch, my head. I can't see anything. What is going on? I am so confused. Are my eyes open? I roll over and start to puke, but it's dark in here, and I have no idea what I am puking on. Or why I am puking. What the heck happened? I try to brush my hair back and find that I am tied up.

Suddenly freaking out now.

"Help!" I try to yell out, but can't yell. My throat hurts. Great, I'm tied up and I can't even call for help. What the heck is going on? Where the fuck am I? I wiggle my feet and legs and find out that my ankles are tied too. But not tight enough to keep me restrained. I begin to wiggle my legs, pulling them up and down and wider to loosen them more. Finally, enough slack formed so I could free my legs. Not so lucky with my hands, they are too tight. They are so tight that they are hurting my wrist.

I need to get out of here. I need to get free.

I try to stand up using the wall behind me to help me stand. I still feel sick and I want to puke again. But I need to get out of here. I don't have time to puke. I struggle as I try to stand.

Thank goodness the wall is behind me to help hold me up. I start to walk along the wall with my back to it, feeling. This is a very difficult task since I can't move fast or run my hands up and down. I have to stand and squat. Which is also making me sicker. I just want to lie back down and go to sleep.

River, stay awake, you need to get out.

I found a door. Yes! I went to open it. NO. It won't open. The door is locked.

"Fuck!" I said as loudly as my voice would let me. I went to move to the middle of the room when I felt something near the door sticking out of the wall. I touch it. It has an edge, kind of. So I rub the ropes along it. I hope this works. I keep rubbing them as fast as I can, but it seems like it takes hours. They break apart, and I shake them and rub my wrist. They hurt, and I can feel the rope marks along them. No time to play around. I gotta get out of here.

My hands are free, so I start to feel the walls again, up and down, looking for some sort of window or another door, something. I need to get out of here. This time, moving more freely and a bit faster, even though I still want to puke. I fell in my dress looking for my phone. Great, lost that too. Thank god I had no money on me when I went to the lounge. I frantically finish running my hands along the wall and then slowly walk around the middle of the room. It's not very big. About the size of a bedroom. Nothing. But then I trip over something. I grabbed it. A brick. I found a brick. What good is that going to do? Wait. I feel my way back to the door I had found and start hitting the knob with the brick. I will break this knob off if I have too.

I hear footsteps coming towards me, and I stop. I can't let them know I am free. What if they give me whatever it was that makes me want to puke? So I sat back down against the wall. With the brick behind my back. The door opens and the light turns on. A nerdy guy walks in. I know he thinks I am tied up. I look him over. He is not very big, not much taller than me. Tiny arms and legs, no real muscle. I could take him. I CAN take him out.

"Well, I am glad to see you are finally awake. I thought it would have worn off a while ago."

A while ago. How long have I been here? What the heck happened?

"A while ago? How long have I been here? And what did you give me?"

"Ah, the questions from the confusion. I didn't give you anything. Jackson did. What a charmer he is, huh?"

"No, not really. I found him to be a bit boring. I mean, if you want the truth." Saying to this guy with a smirk. Which was the truth, from what I can remember.

He walked a little closer, but not close enough to make my attack yet. I need to keep him talking.

"You, on the other hand, I bet you are the charmer. You must have assumed his good looks make him a charmer. And because of that, he could charm me. But honestly, I would have fallen for you over him any day."

He smiled at me. "You are a pretty thing, and smart. I like that."

I smile as if to take the compliment and flirt a little bit. "So, how long have I been here? And why am I here?"

"Three days."

"And it's taken you three days to come see me?" As I bat my eyelashes. I wanted to pop my eyes out when he said that. I have been here for three days. No, that can't be right. Play it cool, play it cool.

I can see his face flush a little. "I have, and you were sleeping so peacefully. I am sorry I had to drug you to get you here. But you seem so distracted and didn't want to talk to us."

"Well, that would be because you didn't come to do the talking. I could have easily been more distracted by you. How about you untie my hands, so we can talk. Maybe bring me some water too." Giving a shy smile and puppy dog eyes at him.

He stood there looking at me, trying to decide what to do. I could tell that I was making him uncomfortable in the excited sort of way.

"I didn't catch your name," I say to him to try and ease the conversation.

"That Ms. Rizzo is because I have not told you."

Ms. Rizzo, here we go again. I have a feeling this has to do with my Dad and his side of the family.

"I think you have me confused with someone else. My name is not Rizzo." I say, still smiling and looking like an innocent schoolgirl.

He looks at me for a while. He still has that look like he wants me, but knows it will jeopardize whatever he is after. He has to adjust himself. After he walks close enough to me that I can make a jump on him. He bends down, which makes it even easier.

"Yes, yes, you are Ms. Rizzo, no need to lie. I don't like it when I am lied to." He reaches out his hand to slap me with a huge grin, and his erection gets harder. This repulses me.

I see it coming. His hand comes towards my face. I pull out the brick and knock him on the head with it. I use all the force I have. I see blood start to pour out of the wound, and he falls to the ground. I feel for a pulse, he still has one. I pat all his pockets. Found keys, his phone, and bingo, my phone.

Fuck who do I text, I have no idea where I am.

Text Cain, Poppy, Noah, and Tatum:

HELP! I was kidnapped and have no idea where I am.

I take off out the door, and there are several hallways. I lock the knob and shut that door just in case. I go down to the right, and there is a double door at the end. I ran to it. I push through it to find another set of doors. They are locked. I pull out the keys and try and see if they work.

One of the keys worked. I opened it and I ended up in an office. No exit door, so I turn to leave, and something catches my eye. I walk over to the desk and see pictures of me. Pictures of me on the bus next to Noah when we stopped the first time. There is also a file marked Ms. Rizzo. I grabbed it all and turned to run out. I got out in the hallway and headed back the way I came from, and I saw a sign that said exit. I ran to it.

I make it to the outside of the building, but I don't see anything else. No other buildings. Nothing. I start running around the building, There has to be a car or something around here. I go around to the other side and find a car sitting there. I run over to it and jump in, and lock the doors. It's a black sedan with tinted windows. I started trying the keys and stayed ducked down so no one could see me inside the car. Finally, I found a key that starts it.

I put it in drive and take off. I see a guy running at me, and I don't slow down. I hit him, but I kept going. I have no idea where, but I get on the road and go the only way I can. I drive until I can't see the building I was at anymore, and I turn. If they come after me, I don't want them to know where I am. I go down a little further and turn again. I want to get space between me and that place. I drive until I come to a city, but no sign of where I am. I find a parking garage and pull into it. I need to call someone, but who?

I grab my phone and have tons of text messages

Poppy: Pumpkin, call me right now.

Noah: Call me

Tatum: Babe, call me

Cain: Call me

Gramma: Darling, call someone, anyone. We need to find out where you are so we can get you.

Just as I was going to dial someone, the phone rang.

"Hello," I frantically yell into the phone.

"Babe, are you OK? Where are you?"

Tatum. As I was going to say something to him, my phone beeps, but I don't change lines. I am already on the phone with him.

"I don't know where I am. In a parking garage"

"Look in your mirrors, do you see anyone?"

"No, just me."

I could hear relief on his end. "OK, I am coming to get you."

"How? You don't know where I am."

He chuckles. "Babe, hell could freeze over and I would still be able to find you."

Aw, I could feel myself blushing. "Is that so, and how would you be able to do that? What if I were frozen in hell?"

He laughs. "Don't you trust me?"

"What makes you think I should trust you?"

"Well, I am coming to rescue you."

I look up and see a car pulling into the garage. "Are you here now?"

"Not yet, why?"

"A car just pulled in."

"River, listen closely to what I tell you to do. Go back out of the garage and turn right." He says it very sternly. It kind of makes me panic. But I have to try and stay calm. Not to mention, I still want to puke.

I put the car in drive and put the phone on speaker so I could drive. "I have you on speaker. I am turning right now."

"Do not use your turn signals. Did the car follow you?"

"Yes, Tatum, I'm scared." I could feel tears leaking out of my eyes. Now is not the time to cry. I feel like I am going to die.

"Babe, it's going to be OK at the next street, turn right."

I turn right. "OK, I just turned."

"You're doing good. Now make a quick left."

I make a quick left. "OK"

"Is the car still behind you?"

"Yes. Yes, the fucking car is still behind me." I yell because right now, I would rather be back in Michigan with my Mom than being chased by some guy who drugged me and kept me tied up for three days. And why the fuck did no one come for me!

"Turn right, right now."

I did, and just as I did, another car comes between me and the car following me and slams on its brakes. I started to stop.

"Don't you dare stop, make the next right and pull down the alley as soon as you turn."

I did exactly what he said to do, and there was a car parked right in the way. I went back up.

"River, get out and get in the other car."

"What the hell?"

"Just do it! NOW!" He yells at me.

I slam the car into park and head to the car in front of me.

The door opens up, and Noah jumps out and grabs me.

Noah, how did he get here? We both dive into the backseat, and the car takes off. I turn to see who is driving. Cain.

"Um, what is going on?" I am really confused.

They look at each other.

"Um, River, hello." I hear it coming from my phone.

Shit, I forgot Tatum was on the phone. "Hey," I picked up the phone. "Can someone explain to me what is going on?"

"Babe, as soon as we get back to the hotel, we will talk to you. I am right behind you."

I turn and see the car that got between me and the car following me behind us.

I sighed.

"OK."

"How are you feeling?"

"Like I am going to puke again."

"Can you take me off speaker phone?"

I look at the guys, and they nod, telling me to do so. I am so confused. How did Noah know Cain and Tatum?

"OK, you're off speaker phone," I say as I put the phone up to my ear.

"OK, Babe. Now I am going to let you go and I want you to rest while we drive back, OK? Noah is going to give you some water, drink it, drink as much as you can."

"OK. See you soon."

"Yes, Babe, you will see me soon." Click on his end, and I set the phone down.

"Here, drink this," Noah hands me water.

I take a drink. "Would you like to explain to me how you know Cain and how you know Tatum? And how come I didn't see you before today? And how long have I been gone? And how come no one even tried to find me?"

Noah lets out a breath. "Cain, Tatum, and I grew up together. We have known each other since we were babies."

"OK, that makes sense," I say, looking at Cain, who is looking at me in the rear-view mirror. His eyes are like I am not sure how to explain, saddened by the fact that I was gone and hurt. And to make sure I was OK. He was making sure I was OK.

I turned to Noah, who was checking out my body. Which I was both flattered and offended by. I hit him in the arm. "Now is not the time to be checking me out."

Cain laughs. Noah rubs his arm. "Hey, Wonder Woman, I was not checking you out. Not that I wouldn't, but I wasn't. I was making sure you were OK. I had time to check on you on the bus."

He must have gotten some of those truth pills. Now I feel myself blush, and I turn away from him and glance at the mirror, and see a smile on Cain's face. I knew he was now in agreement. UGH.

I lay my head on the window and stare out at the sky. Noah reaches over and pulls me into him.

"At least be comfortable while you lie."

It was nice lying on him instead of the window. But won't Cain tell Tatum, and what will Tatum think? Oh, all this thinking is making my head hurt. And what if Tatum can see us through the back window? I think my life just got more complicated. I see Cain looking at me, but not like he was mad or that he was going to tell Tatum, more like he wished I was lying on him. Maybe AnnaB was right. Maybe I need to date them all and kind of let nature take its course.

But would they agree to it?

20

Tatum's Report

Cain has been trying to triangulate the signal from her cell for the last twenty-four hours. How could I be so stupid? I should have just come over, even though she was meeting someone. Well, now I know she was meeting Noah. Where the fuck was he when this all happened.

Stop yelling at yourself. It wasn't like Noah knew this was going to happen. Security footage shows a guy approach her, and you can tell she isn't interested, and he sits down anyway. He gets up and buys a drink, and slips in something pink in color. She had no idea it was in there. She drinks it slowly, and her facial expressions show that she is bored. Then she stands up and looks like she is going to pass out. The guy grabs her and says something to a worker, and takes off the back doors. He picked up her phone on the way, but what we keep getting is the Grand Canyon area, but no pinpoint to where. And that place is huge. Zeke and Mykayla went out and drove around to see what they could find a couple of times, but nothing where the signal was coming from.

"What are we going to tell Mr. Rizzo?" I hear Cain ask.

"The truth," I hear Jazmine say to him. "I have already spoken with him. He said if we don't hear something or find her in the next twenty-four hours, he is flying in."

"It's been three days already what the fuck does this guy want with her?" I walk over and punch the wall. Which makes Jazmine laugh.

"What the heck is so funny?" I turned to her. I want to punch her now. I can't because she is higher up in rank than me. This circle is her circle. It's hard to believe she has been doing this for so long that she has a circle at the young age of eighteen.

"Nothing about this," she points to all the monitors, "but you, my friend, like this girl." She says, smirking.

"She is our target. It is my job to keep her safe. And so far, we have failed at this. What the fuck are we going to do?" I knew what she meant. I was starting to like this girl. But I am not sure if she likes me. And I know Noah and Cain like her, too. But why couldn't she just tell me she was meeting a guy?

"Yup, keep saying that," Jazmine says to me, laughing. "It's not like we thought this was going to happen. And who is this guy anyway? Any pings on him?"

Ping. My phone, Cain's phone, and Noah's all go off. Before we can all read them, Jazmine's goes off from Mr. Rizzo.

"Triangulate her cell now!" Jazmine orders. Zeke walks in, and she points to him and to where Cain is. "Cain, you and Noah in one car, Tatum, you in another. KK, you follow, stay back for backup. Zeke, you stay and pinpoint where it is coming from. Mykayla, if you are needed, jump into action; otherwise, stay behind and do what we need you to do."

We all jump into action.

I keep texting her, and I am not getting another message. Come on, River, pick up your phone and text me back.

I have to call her. I pick up my phone and dial her number.

"Hello," she screams into the phone.

That's not good, something has happened to her. Hurry up, Zeke, find her.

"Babe, are you OK? Where are you?" I need to calm her down so we can get her. I've got to keep her on the phone. I need to stay calm.

21

Their Kiss

I must have fallen asleep because the next thing I remember was having Tatum pick me up off Noah's lap, and I opened my eyes. I was freaked out that I was just on Noah's lap, and Tatum is now seeing that. I am unsure how he will react to it.

"Wonder Woman, we are home. You don't have to open your eyes. Tatum is going to carry you in."Awe, Noah's soothing voice. I could have sworn he just kissed my forehead, but I can't open my eyes. I love the sound of his voice. It reminds me of the bus ride here.

We got back to the room, and I was lying on something. It didn't feel like my bed. I open my eyes and see the guys standing there, not paying attention to me talking among themselves. I can't hear what they are saying. I see that I am in the living room. I got up and ran to the bathroom.

I barely made it there and puked. I felt like shit. But I did get drugged. The guys all come running into the bathroom, finding me on the floor next to the toilet. This made me cry. I didn't want them to see me like this. And I didn't want them to think I was helpless. Because I will not be helpless. I have never been helpless, and I am not about to start.

Cain was the first one to come to me. He wrapped me up in his arms, telling me that everything was going to be OK. I had my head up on his chest, and the tears kept coming. I didn't even know why I was crying, but he started to rock me. He kept rubbing up and down my back, trying to soothe me.

When I was finally able to stop crying, Noah handed me a glass of water and a couple of pills. I took the water but didn't want to take the pills. I mean, I had just been drugged.

"Babe, these pills will help flush whatever is in your system faster." I hear Tatum say. I turned and looked at him, realizing I was still in Cain's arms, and at that point, I didn't even care. I took the pills.

"Are you able to get undressed, or do you need help? We have a bath run for you." Aw, how sweet of Cain. Wait, we?

I looked at each of the guys, and they just kept looking at me with concern. "I think I would rather take a shower. I don't want to fall asleep in the tub."

This made them laugh, and Tatum started the shower. I got up and got undressed, not even aware that they were all in there, or not even caring at that point, not sure which. I stood in the shower for a while. I liked the way it was feeling on my body. I washed my hair and my body. And was still standing there letting it wake me up. I grab a towel and wrap my hair up. I shut off the water, feeling like a new person. I step out of the shower. And reach for another towel.

OK, I keep ending up in these very awkward situations. I have to say, this is not normal. Up until I left for Vegas, I never had this kind of stuff happen. Maybe I was better off with Dylan and skipping the bus. Shoot, I was supposed to text him and tell him I was OK. River, back to reality now. Earth to River.

Anyway, I step out of the shower, and bam. Three hot guys are staring at me. Once again, I am naked and have someone looking at me. Very awkward. And this time it was all three of them.

"Do you want to take a picture? I mean it will last longer, and you can stop watching me shower." I say to them being a smart ass. Big mistake.

I see them all look at one another, and big smiles come across their faces. I see them shrug, and all three of them reach for their phones.

I hurry up and wrap my towel around myself.

"I was kidding!" I say to them.

I hear clicks. Thank God I have a towel on.

"You delete those at once!" I yell at them.

"You have a picture of me on your phone," Cain says to me. "It's only fair I have one."

I look over at him and see that smirk on his face, and I want to go punch him again. I want to punch him so bad right now.

"You all delete that pic of me in my towel. And you can have a pic of me in my clothes. Or I will punch you and delete the pics after you drop your phone, and you will not get a pic later." I storm out of the bathroom, giving them time to decide. Turning to give them a serious look and I was not going to give them much time to decide.

"OK, we will delete the pic." I hear Noah say to me, and see all the guys shaking their heads yes.

I turn back around and smile to myself. "Now I am going to my room to get dressed." I start to walk, and I hear footsteps following me.

I turn around and see them following me. I put up my hand to stop them. "I do not need help getting dressed."

"Well, the last time we saw you, you needed two hot gods to dress you. Wouldn't three be better?"

Oh, Cain. I shake my head and look down at the floor. Noah's eyes are wide open, staring at me, then at Cain, as if to get some sort of response from one of us.

"Not today, I will take a rain check." I looked each of the guys in their eyes, one after the other, seeing if I could weigh out what they were thinking. And there was no real reaction. Shrugs, and they walk away.

I open the door to my room and find all the pics I had been looking at in a big pile on the bed, not spread out anymore. And the box had the lid back on it. I was so sad when I saw that pic of my Mom again. And it makes me cry. I put the stuff back in the box, except for that pic of my Mom, and moved the box to the corner of the room, not wanting to go through them. I lay on the bed, still in my towel, crying, looking at the pic. I curl up in a ball holding that pic to my chest.

Why can't my Mom be like this now? Why did she have to use drugs? I start to wonder what things would have been like had she not been into drugs. Would she have ever met my Dad? Why couldn't she be clean now? What was making her hate me so much that she had to hurt herself and make me suffer? I couldn't stop crying, and I was feeling numb.

Oh, did I fall asleep again? I open my eyes, and the room is dark. I am not holding the pic anymore. I stretch my body out and yawn. I wonder how long I've been asleep. I ended up hitting two people. Um, what the heck. I turn to my right and I see Cain. I turn to my left and I see Tatum. I have two guys in my bed, and I am in the middle. I sit up a little bit to check out the room, and I see Noah next to Cain. I took that back, and all three of them were in bed with me. I look down, and I am in a t-shirt and panties. Well, at least they covered me with clothes. I look at the shirt. Noah's. It has Superman on it.

I was looking at Tatum, and he opened his eyes. Caught again staring. He smiles. "How are you feeling?" He whispers to me.

"Better than earlier. Still a bit tired." I whispered back to him.

"Yeah, the tiredness will be from the drugs in your system. What's wrong?"

I feel tears again on my face. How can he make me feel so comfortable talking to him? And how did he know that something was wrong? I hate that these guys seem to know me. Sometimes better than I know myself.

He picks me up off the bed and carries me out of the room. Confused about what was going on, I let him.

He sits me on the couch and leaves the room. He comes back a few minutes later with a blanket and some water. I take a drink of the water, and I can feel the tears still in my eyes.

"Would you like to tell me why you're crying?" He softly asks me. He sits down and covers me up, and pulls me into his chest. If this had been the other day, I would want to lick it. And kiss him, not that I don't want to now, but I was crying like a baby.

"My Dad gave me a box with files in it. I opened it before I was kidnapped, and I found a file with pictures of my Mom, my Mom and some guy, and of my Mom and Dad. The first picture I found was when my Mom was like sixteen. She was so innocent and sweet. She was beautiful. Why didn't I get the chance to know my Mom like that? Why couldn't I have a Mom who even cared a little bit?"

I know there was no answer to the question, but it felt better saying it. He hugged me and held me tight in his arms while I cried. I knew that he was just going to listen to whatever I had to say. "I think the guy in the pictures with my Mom is a guy named Roman, and she thinks he kidnapped me."

"Why do you think she thinks that?"

"She said something to me when she called. I don't know what to think. I don't even know what is true in my past."

He just keeps rubbing his hand up and down my back. I didn't want to talk anymore, and my crying had started to stop. My eyelids get heavy, and they close.

I woke up back in my bed. How do they do that? Move me without me knowing they move me. I roll over, expecting to see Tatum, but I see Cain. Ah, Tatum must be on the other side of me. Nope, it's Noah. He has his arm around me. OK, I sit up a little, looking for Tatum, and he isn't in here. That's weird. I lay back down, I am turned with my back up against Noah and facing Cain. He opens his eyes.

Of course he does. It's like these guys have a sixth sense and can tell when I am looking at them. He smiles, and I start to blush.

"I like it when you blush."

What does he try to do and make me blush on purpose? Which makes me blush even more. He smiles. He scoots me closer to him. I am very aware that Noah's hand is still on my hip, and now Cain's is on my waist.

"You are so beautiful."

OK, I know I am blushing again. Mostly, I am starting to turn red.

He leans in and lightly places his lips on mine. They are so soft. I let him kiss me. His tongue comes out of his mouth and teases my lips, and I open my mouth slightly, and he lets his tongue come into my mouth. He kisses me a little harder and a lot more passionately. We are both teasing each other with our tongues. I take hold of his lip, and he kisses me hard. He tastes so good. I trace his lips with my tongue and tease him with it. He kisses a little bit harder, then a lot softer. He pulls away. Stares at me. I start to blush again. He leans in and kisses me again.

"I have to get up." He says to me and rolls out of bed, leans down, and kisses me again. When he stands up, I notice he is already up. Which makes me smile. But he didn't see me look, or see me smile at it.

I wasn't ready to get up, so I lay there working on waking up. I scoot myself a little bit closer to Noah just so I could be cuddling with someone. I didn't want to be alone. I mean, I know I am not alone with the guys here, but I needed to feel Noah next to me.

I hear him moan a little bit in his sleep and talk. I couldn't make out what he was saying, though. He wiggles around and next thing I know I have a hand on my boob and I am being pulled in even closer to him. I try to look to see if he is awake, but he's not. Nice, we haven't even kissed, and he's just going to skip bases. I laugh a little bit to myself.

I lay there for a while, thinking I should get up and call Poppy. Just then Noah wakes up, feels his hand on my boob and sits up and yanks his hand back. He turns to me with this I can't believe I did that look on his face. Which makes me burst out in laughter.

He smiles and lies back down. "I'm sorry about that."

"About what? Grabbing me in your sleep?"

"Well, yeah."

"It's OK."

He smiles and leans in and kisses me. Whoa, another kiss while the other two guys are right out that door? Not even that long since Cain kissed me? Things are awkward and weird. I don't even know how I feel about all this.

His kiss starts slow and desperate. I am not sure why it would be desperate. It's like he has been wanting this for too long. He licks my lips and traces them with his tongue. I follow his lead. He doesn't go right for my mouth and teases my tongue with his. He wraps his arms around me and pulls me closer to him. The urge to feel me next to him, I want that, and I can tell he wants that too. He rubs his hands down my back till he gets to the bottom of the shirt. He grabs my ass and pulls me into his groin area. I can feel his hardness against my body. Rubbing on me. Exciting me. He runs his hands up the back of my shirt and pulls it up to expose my breast. But not off. He stops kissing my lips and takes his lips to my nipple and starts teasing it with his tongue. Then lightly sucking on it. Then he switches to the other one and does the same. I could cut a window with how hard they are right now. I can feel that my panties are soaking wet right now. And I am sure he can feel it too. He comes back to my lips and kisses me this time deep and hard as he holds and caresses my breast. He lets go of my boobs and slowly slows his kiss. Then stops.

Seriously? Not this again. Why does this continue to happen to me? I mean, I am not sure if I am ready to have sex with any of them, but why do they continue to do this to me?

"My God, why do you do this to me?"

"Do what?" Does he not know what he does to me?

He grabs my hand and rubs it on his Johnson. "This!"

I kind of smile. I like that. He lets go and sits up. No! Don't sit up. He leans back over and kisses me once again.

"We have to get up, and you need to eat. It has been like four days since you have eaten." He gets up, finds his pants, and readjusts himself. He waves at me to get up.

"Fine, but give me a minute to get dressed, and I will meet you out there."

"OK, but hurry."

I nod, and he leaves. I have to change; I cannot go out there with these panties on. I climb out of bed and get dressed.

I walk out, and I hear Poppy. I run to the dining room and, with a bit of disappointment, I only see Poppy on the TV. I was hoping he would have been here.

"Pumpkin, how are you feeling?"

"Better now, Poppy. I miss you and love you."

"I love you, too. I see you have some friends over." He says that smiling at me.

I start to blush, and he laughs. "Pumpkin, I know these guys. I trust them. Until we can figure out who took you, I want to have one of them stay with you at all times. I don't want you to be alone. Will that be OK with you?"

Duh. I think to myself. I see Gramma. She walks to the camera, "Oh darling, I am so glad you are OK. I love you. Check your phone. I sent you a message. And speaking of phone, we got you a new one, your other one was bugged."

"What about my numbers? What do you mean bugged? How are we going to find out who took me?"

I hear Cain behind me, "All the important ones have been put in your new phone."

I turn around and look at them. "What do you all know about what is going on?"

"Pumpkin, they only know what I have told them. Tell me about your kidnapping."

"All I remember was being at the lounge waiting for, um." Do I tell them it was Noah?

"We already know it was Noah, Pumpkin."

Like Poppy, always reading my mind. "Some guy came over with horrible pickup lines. I told him I wasn't interested, but he sat anyway. Asked if he could buy me a drink, I told him a bottle of water, and he came back with something else. Next thing I know, I am in a dark room, tied up and puking. I got my feet loose and found something to cut my hands free with. I found a brick and was trying to break the lock on the door when I heard footsteps. I sat back down, and some guy came in. A different guy. I had the brick behind my back, and when he went to slap me, I hit him with it. It knocked him out, and his head was bleeding. Then I got out, and you know the rest. The guy at the Lounge, his name was Jackson, the other guy I don't know." I think I summed it up "Shit!"

"Shit what?" Everyone said in unison.

"I found a file with a picture of me and Noah in it. I grabbed it, but I am not sure where it went."

Cain looked at me, then at Poppy. "I found it in the car and brought it in, I haven't looked at it yet, sir."

Why is he calling my Poppy, sir?

"Very well, let me know. River, you understand you have to have one of the guys with you at all times, right?"

"Yes, Poppy, but I don't want a babysitter for the rest of my life."

"You won't, dear." I hear Gramma say.

"Love you guys, I need to eat."

"We love you, too, Pumpkin."

The line disconnects. I sit down, and there is already a plate of food ready for me. I smile.

"Can I have my phone? I need to check my message from Gramma."

Cain hands it to me. I picked up some bacon and put it in my mouth.

My mouth drops open. Did my Gramma just text that to me? Not Gramma.

OH. MY. GOD.

22

Shopping

Text from Gramma: River, dear. I know you're dealing with a lot. And a little birdie told me you are struggling with liking more than one boy. Noah, Cain, and Tatum are all very nice-looking and very available guys. They are very different from any others. If I were young like you and in your situation. I would do them all. But don't tell Poppy. He would get jealous. Have fun while you're young. I wish things were like they were when I was younger, because I would have had more fun being young. Live a little. And don't forget to tell me about it. BTW (Yup, Gramma is working on text talk) Grandma agrees! <3 you dear.

I was still in shock with the message I just read, so I didn't even hear the guys talking to me. I just stared at the phone. What the heck, Gramma? Did she send that message to me? I reread it. Yup she sure did. Wow my Gramma would have been the woman back in the day.

I think about what my Gramma would be like when she was younger and starting to date Poppy. I have seen pics of her when she was younger. Very beautiful. She had long flowing black hair and dark eyes. Nice, beautiful facial structure. She had such a beautiful smile. She still has that smile. It turns heads, that's for sure. I could not picture my Gramma with anyone but my Poppy. He was a very handsome man. My Dad looked a lot like him. Tall, dark, and handsome. Poppy is over six feet, with dark, dark-toned skin and very well built. Most of the time, my Poppy can put a twenty-year-old to shame with his body. Gramma got lucky when she found him. My Dad, from what I remember, was a lot of Poppy. Very handsome men.

Thinking about this made tears start to form in my eyes. I wish that I could have my Dad right now. I really miss him. Over the last eight years, I have been so strong and brave, but I have yet to face the issues that I have lost my Dad. I cried the day of his funeral, but then it was because I was never going to see him again. After that, with my Mom using drugs the day of the funeral and every day since, I have had to put on a brave face, and a brave me. I mean, I couldn't grieve because if I did, well, who was going to take care of Mom?

Maybe if I had known what was going on with my Dad and the drug lords, I could have saved him. Maybe he would still be alive if I had done something different. Why does my Mom have to be the way she is? This is not how I want my life to be. I didn't sign up for this. I need to do something. I need to help my Mom and catch this guy that killed my Dad, and that is killing my Mom. I have to do this before he kills me.

I stop crying and snap back to what is going on around me.

I have three sets of eyes staring at me.

"Babe, are you OK?" Tatum speaks up.

I smirk, grab a piece of bacon, and shove it into my mouth. "Yup, I'm just peachy." I grab more food. And eat some more. I am processing a game plan in my head. "How do I talk to Poppy on that TV like I did earlier?"

The exchange looks, and Cain gets up. He walked to the remote that was sitting on the TV. "You push this button." I see a connection thing on the screen.

"Is there something else you need?" I hear Poppy on the screen.

This makes me smile. "Yes, Poppy, I needed to know how to call you."

He laughs and shakes his head. "You have a phone, pumpkin."

"I know, but sometimes I want to see you too."

"Did they show you how to do it?"

"Yes, Poppy, Cain just did. I love you. I am going to finish eating now. Tell Gramma I love her, too. Oh, can I use this to call Gramma when I need some advice, and it's just me and her?"

"Of course, dear." I hear Gramma.

I smile at her as she walks up. "Thanks, Gramma. I love you guys."

"Love you too," they both say as they hang up the call.

I turn and sit back down. "I can do that with anyone?"

"If they have a laptop or TV with a camera, then yes. Why do you want to know?" I hear Noah say to me.

"Just in case I want to talk to AnnaB, or my Grandma, or other people," I say, smiling.

"What other people?" Tatum asks me.

"Oh, this guy Dylan." I knew Noah had heard about him. But I had not mentioned him to the other two.

They all stare at me, which makes me blush and feel happy inside. I lose it and I start laughing. "Don't worry about it, boys, I'm not interested in him. I was kidding."

I push myself away from the table and get up to go back to my room. I need to shower and make a list of things I am going to do. I am lost in thought when I feel an arm around me.

I turn and see Cain.

"Beautiful, are you OK?"

For once, I was OK. But I needed to be alone. "Yeah, I am better than fine. But I am going to shower and do a few things in my bedroom alone. Is that OK?"

Tatum walks over to me, picks me up and puts his hands on my ass, like he always does and naturally I wrap my legs around him. He leans in and kisses me. Not as deeply and passionately as before, but it was still intense. As he sits me down, he tells me he has to go to work. He would text me later to check in. I agree with him with a nod.

Noah walks over, leans down, and kisses me. A lot like Tatum. It was a bit weird to have him kiss me, and the others not throwing a punch. It made me a bit tense, but not too tense to give myself over to Noah. He tells me he has to get to work, too. I am still confused about what he does. I figure I would ask another time. I was on a mission.

Both guys left the room, and Cain came up behind me and picked me up. "So, it's just me and you today. What are we going to do?"

I already had a plan on what I wanted to do. But I guess I can have him tag along. I mean, I can't be alone, right? I can feel myself start to smile at the thought.

"First, I am going to shower, then I have a few things I want to do. You can join me after my shower."

"How about I join you in the shower?" He smirks at me.

"Not today. Sorry. But I would like some hot cocoa if you would get me some for when I get out of the shower?"

"Your wish is my command, my princess."

I laugh and get in the shower. While I was in the shower, I thought about everything. Let the old me wash down the drain and work on the new me. I am going to leave this shower a new River. I finish up and get out and wrap myself up in the towels. I brush my teeth while I am in the bathroom and head to my room.

I find some clothes and work on looking to see if I have workout clothes. I do not. Hmm. I have a few things that I have to do. Then I can work on finding out who this guy is after my Mom and possibly me.

I walk over to my desk and start up my laptop.

Just then, Cain comes back in with my cocoa. "Here you are, my lady."

I chuckle and take it, and he sits down in the chair next to the desk.

"Cain, I am going to need to go shopping after I do a few things on the laptop. I need to pick up a few things."

"OK," he says without questioning me.

I get online and order my Grandma a laptop and a camera, and use the card that my Dad gave me. Then it dawns on me that I have no idea how much is on this. I look at the card closely, and it says a bank name on it. I looked that up online, and there happens to be one here in Vegas. I walk over to my backpack and grab out a pen and paper. While looking through my bag, I found the present from Grandma. I forgot about it.

I opened it up. First, there is a key. Unknown what it is for. Second is a check for ten grand. This was supposed to pay for my first year of college. There is a note.

Dear River, Use the money for what is needed. If you do need it. Secondly, you will learn what the key is for and when you do.

Just remember, we love you.

Grandma and Papi (Mom's parents, even though Papi has passed on)

I wonder what the key is for. But I don't need it right now. I take the check and put it with the rest of the money I have. I go to the computer and start making a list.

List:

Work out wear

Go to the Bank

Open an account

Find someone to teach me more self-defense

"I know just the person." I forgot that Cain was in here.

I turn around and swing, but miss as he was expecting it.

"Why are you snooping?"

"I wasn't just seeing what all we have to do. Are you ready?"

I get up, walk over to the closet, and grab a purse. I put in the key from Grandma, the credit card from Gramma, the check, and the cash I have. I also grab my birth certificate, social security card, and license. Still unsure about the key.

"Yup, I'm ready."

We walk out to the car and get in. We have about twenty-five minutes to get to the bank. So we have time to talk on the way.

"So, Cain. Ummm."

I was lost for words.

He smirks. "So, River." He just stares at me, then back at the road. "Favorite color?"

What? Really?

"Pink, and yours? And do you know Noah's and Tatum's, too?" Doh, why did I ask that?

"I like Blue, Noah likes Green, and Tatum likes Purple."

"I want to learn self-defense so I can take care of myself just in case, I don't want to end up like I was before." I just blurt it out. "I don't care what anyone says. You either agree to it, or you don't, but I will still do it."

"I agree."

"Thank you," I whisper to him.

I quickly sent a text to AnnaB and Grandma letting them know I am OK. I mean, it's been several days.

"We have let your Grandma know about your situation. Well, Mrs. Rizzo has been talking to her."

I had already figured as much. "Do you know anything about my Mom?"

"Only what you have told someone. I do believe I heard she was in rehab."

"Yeah, my Grandma put her in one. I want to make sure she is safe there. How can I find this out?"

He looked at me, confused as to why I would want to do that. "I will help you when we get back home."

I was also sitting here thinking. I wonder if Roberto was in on the whole me getting attacked at dinner with Poppy. I will have to make sure I don't use him until I know for sure. I jot it down in the note.

We pull into the bank. I go in and go to the counter and explain who I am. They pulled up the account for me and told me I could just continue to use this one, and I deposited the money into the account. The lady told me I also had a safe deposit box if I needed to store stuff in it. Wow, I was surprised. I asked if there had been anything put in there. And she said she was unsure, as this account is old. I told her I would come back with stuff I wanted to store in there. She printed off a receipt with my balance on it. I looked at it, then at her, and asked her if that was right, and she assured me it was.

I have never seen so many zeros behind a number before. I wouldn't have to ever work. Maybe I should buy the hotel. I was so stunned that I just stuck it in my purse.

We finished my list, I mean we went shopping, OK. First, we went to an office supply store. I needed a printer. I grabbed a printer with Cain's help. I also grabbed some paper and pens, and a few more things for my desk I needed. I wanted a safe for some things to be kept safe in my room. So Cain helps me pick out something.

"Cain, can I buy some things for my room? Make it a little bit more mine?"

"You can buy anything you want, beautiful."

He drove me to a home decor store. I go crazy inside this store. As I am walking around, I notice a lady. I had seen her at the other stores earlier today as well. I just blew it off and continued to shop. I found a chair that looks like a high-heeled shoe. It is bright pink and zebra print. I want that.

"Cain, I want that."

He starts laughing at me. "Really?"

"Yes, I really do."

Cain goes and gets someone to come help us. He told the person to follow us around and have someone gather all the stuff I want. This was the first time I have ever been able to shop like this. I found a bright pink princess chair for the vanity in the bathroom. I found a bedding set that is bright pink, zebra, and giraffe print. I found like ten pillows. I find some that I can have names added to. I grab one in bright pink and have them add River to it. Then, a blue one and have them add Cain to it. Green for Noah and purple for Tatum.

I feel pretty satisfied with the bedding stuff and walking to where the candles, frames, and pictures are. I found some picture frames and some candles. Oh, do I need curtains? What else do I need? No, I don't need curtains. But I do need some clothes and some make up and bathroom stuff.

"I think I am ready."

"Are you sure?" Cain asked me.

"Yup." I pay for the stuff, and we head to buy some makeup.

I go in and pick out makeup. I found some perfume and some shower stuff I needed. I was looking at some purses when, once again, I saw the same lady. This is getting to be a bit weird. I check out and I know I need to go buy some clothes, so we head that way.

I get into the store and I start browsing. I need workout shorts, yoga pants, sports bras, and some tennis shoes. I found some really cute pink running shoes. Yup, these are the ones I think to myself. I start picking out shorts and spandex, and sports bras. I look up and see that woman again. Now I know she is following me. I have never seen her before today, and every store I went into, she was there.

"Cain, can we go get ice cream across the street?" I whispered to him so no one else could hear me.

He leans in, kisses my ear, and says, "Yeah, let's go check out."

We checked out, and the lady is still shopping but watching. We walk out and walk across the street, order our ice cream, and sit down. That lady follows us there. I take out my phone, and pretend to take a selfie and snap a pic of that lady.

I sent it to Cain. With a text attached, this lady has been following us.

He shakes his head in understanding and sends a message back: Finish eating, I have a plan in the works.

We sat there pretending to be on a date and had more small

talk. He prefers dogs over cats. Likes to swim, and listens to all types of music.

He stands up and reaches for my hand, our backs are turned towards the lady following us, and we head out the door and walk to a car that is not his. He opens the door, and I get in. He gets in the front, and I turn and see Noah driving.

I sign out relief, and he pulls out.

"Good eye." Noah smiles at me. "We are running her picture as we speak."

"Who is?" I ask.

I mean, it seems weird that these guys are always free and happen to know how to find a bug. I am beginning to wonder who all these guys are as well.

"We are," Noah repeats.

"Can you tell me how?"

"With the software we have at home." He says. He sounds like he is unsure of what he can tell me. "Zeke is running the picture through a database."

"Who is Zeke?"

They look at each other as if they need to tell me something, but are unsure if they are allowed to.

I sort of feel like I am on my own to bring down Roman and save my Mom. I was unable to save my Dad. I will be damned if I let my Mom die too. I know she wasn't a good Mom, but no one needs to die because of some criminal who makes a living selling drugs.

We ride the rest of the way back in silence, not wanting to break the mood. Besides, I am lost in my thoughts anyway.

I head outside when we get back to the hotel. I walk and lie on the chair and look up at the night sky. Not that it is very dark with all the lights, but I could see some stars. As I was lying there thinking about everything.

"She says nothing at all, but simply stares upward into the dark sky and watches, with sad eyes, the slow dance of the infinite stars." I hear someone say behind me.

I turn and see Noah.

"Stardust, by Neil Gaiman," I reply to him

"Ah, you have read it."

I smile and nod. As he comes closer to me and kisses me. A slow, deep, tender kiss. His tongue feels my lips, and I feel his. When we finally come up for air, I tell him I need to head to my room and do a few things. He tells me OK. That they would start dinner.

I walk into my room and find my stuff there. Confused, I walk back out of the room, and I can hear Tatum. That explains it. I smile. I decided I need to "redo" my room. I turn on some music and start to put away my clothes. I pick up my safe and stick it in the corner next to the dresser and the wall. I move the chair that is in there out to the hallway between the door to my room and the main living space of the hotel. It fits nicely there. I go back into my room and grab the high-heeled chair I bought today and put it in the now open spot. It looks good there, if I do say so myself. I hooked up the printer and put away all my desk stuff. I pull out my bedding stuff and start to make my bed. Ah, nice new sheets and bedding. I have never had new bedding before, and it feels so wonderful. I pull out the last pillow case, and an envelope falls out.

What the hell? What is that?

I opened it.

OH! MY! GOODNESS!

23

Too Many Questions

I am still staring at the contents of the package. When I hear a knock at the door. I shove it under the pillows on the bed.

Tatum walks in. He starts laughing as he looks around.

"So why did you get pillows with our names on them?"

That is an easy response, but do I tell him the truth? "Because if you are going to start staying here, you need your pillows."

That makes him laugh even more. He walks over and gently kisses me. "It's time for dinner."

I am unsure if I should tell them about the package I found. I am not even sure how it got there. I think I should wait. Besides, I want to see what it is first.

"OK." I get up and follow him out to the dining area. YUMMY! I want to just stay in my bedroom and figure out what all that was about. "It looks so delicious, and smells so good too." I think to myself, I need to hurry up and get back in the bedroom so I can figure out what that package is all about.

I sit down and take a couple of bites of food. Oh, it's like heaven in your mouth. It is chicken, grilled and seasoned just right. And a salad with fried potatoes and steamed carrots. It was the best food I have ever tasted! I am not even exaggerating a little bit.

"I told Cain I want to learn more self-defense. And he agreed with me. Now I am telling you the same. I do not want to end up in a situation like before, and if by chance I do. I want to make sure I can take care of myself. If someone is after me. I want to make sure I can hold my own. Is this understood?"

I don't know what took over me as far as telling them what I was going to do. My tone was more bossy than it had ever been before. They never did anything before that that would make me think they wouldn't be OK with it. But I am just so confused about what is going on. And who these guys are. And everything for that matter. I am not even sure who I am. I am glad I bought that journal because now more than ever I need to write everything I do know down.

I notice all the guys are in agreement with me on the self-defense training. Good, I am glad that went easily because I am unsure if the rest of this will go as easily.

"I think Roberto might have been part of me getting attacked during the dinner with Poppy, and maybe even for me getting kidnapped. I do not want to use him anymore. And since your cars all seem to be known, I am thinking I need to get my car. For us, a new one that will throw off whoever is after me. We might need more than one. Besides, I want my car. I am sick of you guys driving me everywhere." I say with a smirk.

"What? Do we drive that badly?" said Noah with a look of disappointment on his face.

"Um, it is not that. Sometimes a girl likes to drive. Well, I mean this girl likes to drive. I have always, well, been on my own, and sometimes I just have to be in control of myself. I have been feeling sort of helpless since I left home."

"We will see." I hear Cain say. He sounded like that was what I wanted to hear, but they weren't going to let me do it.

"No, we won't see, we will do. This is not me asking. Either you help me, or I will do it on my own."

"You heard your grandpa, you are not allowed to go anywhere without one of us." I turn and see that Noah is speaking up again. What is it with these guys? Are they trying to control me?

"Really? I did hear that. But last time I checked, I was an adult. I am over the age of eighteen, and I have been taking care of myself for the last eight years. You weren't around until now. I can be on my own without any of you. I am sure if I call my Gramma, she would agree that I need a car." I am royally pissed right now and I am about to get up and just leave. Leave the hotel and go out on my own. I have enough money to buy a house and stay hidden forever. I could move to another country, and no one would ever find me. But these three have started to grow on me.

No one says anything else about the car for right now. But this is going to get a huge response. "I want a handgun, too!" I just came out with it. I pick up some more food and take a bite. I do have to say this food is so good.

"HELL NO!" This time, it is Tatum who says it. The one that has been so quiet through all of this just stood up, slammed his hands down on the table, and yelled. "You don't need a gun. Do you even know how to use a gun? You could shoot one of us or worse, yourself."

I blow out my breath. "I am getting one. I will learn how to use it. It is as simple as that." I turn to look at each one of the guys with a very serious I am not taking any shit look on my face. "This is not up for discussion either." I take another bite of my food and melt into heaven again.

"I don't agree." I hear them say.

"I didn't ask if you did. I wasn't asking for permission. I was simply telling you what I was going to do."

"We will not allow you to get a gun."

Allow? Did they just say allow it? When did I become a child, and did they become a parent? That is it! I have had enough of them thinking they are my boss. And from what I can see, my Poppy is their boss.

I get up and walk over to the TV and call Poppy.

"Hello, did something happen?" I hear Poppy say.

"Poppy! I miss you!"

"Oh, pumpkin, what is wrong? I miss you too!"

"OK, first, I think Roberto might have something to do with me being kidnapped and what happened at our dinner." I see him nod his head.

"That is a great idea, pumpkin. Is that why you called me?"

"Nope, but I wanted you to know that as well. I called because I have told these three idiots what I want to happen." I see Poppy staring at me, then looks at each of the guys with a look of what the heck. "I want to take self-defense. They all agree that it is a good idea. Also, we were followed again today. I want my own car. I think they know these morons' cars and I think a few new ones would be nice. I also think I need a handgun. But I am told HELL NO by all of them. I told them I wasn't asking. Either we do this, and let me have a say over my own life. Or I will be leaving."

I see Poppy smiling. What is it with everyone smiling like I am crazy? I mean, this is my life, and I guess it is too big of a risk here. I blow out my breath and wait. Either he will tell them to listen to me, or I am out. End of story.

After what seemed like a lifetime, I see Poppy shaking his head in defeat. But the look on his face didn't show defeat. It showed something else. Happiness? He looked like he was proud. That was not what I was expecting.

"This is what is going to happen, so you four had better listen carefully." We all shake our heads. "Jazmine and Mykayla will take River for a gun, and they will teach her to shoot it. They will come for her soon. Their work is almost done. Zeke will take her to pick out a few cars. Self-defense will start tomorrow. River, pumpkin, will you please listen to these three? They are not out to make you go crazy. They do want to keep you safe. Please?"

Aw, he seems so worried. "Yes, Poppy, I will, but they need to understand that I need to be me, too. I have not had someone watching over me since I was ten. I have been on my own, and the one parent in my life back in Michigan was more my child than I was hers. I don't want to be tied down and not do anything. I will leave and change my name and do whatever it takes to be free."

Poppy starts laughing. "Pumpkin, I get you. Now I need to have a few words with the guys alone, please?"

I nod and get up to leave, but first, I grab my food. I close the door enough that they can't see me. And I stay put. If they are going to talk about me, I want to know what they are saying.

"River needs to be trained. CamCade trained. It is going to be in her best interest if she is brought in, but we can't do it till we locate Roman. We need to find out what Roman wants. He has located Rosalie. We have her in detox treatment. Zeke has been dumping all calls made to and from Rosalie. How come I was not aware that you guys were being followed, and what did you find out about the guy that took her?"

I begin to wonder what CamCade is. And why are they trying to find Roman? What could he possibly want? What does he want with my Mom?

"The guy from the Lounge, we found out his name is Jackson, so he didn't lie about that. He seems to have no ties to Roman. So we are unsure what is going on with that. Does someone else want River, too?" I hear Noah say.

"As far as we know. Possibly. I mean, Agent Parker had many big cases. We need to review all of them. Jazmine and Macky have been to the site where they kept River. There was nothing there. Some blood in a little room and a brick. They are running DNA now. Will keep you posted."

Parker was my Dad. I need to find out what cases he had worked on in order to figure out why everyone is after me.

I walked away. It was too much to take in.

I get back to my room and pick up the stuff I found in the pillow. I set the plate down and took a few more bites. I find a letter and start to read it.

River,

Well, at least that is what you're called. I am trying to save you, but I see you ran away from me. That boy would not leave you alone, so I could come to you. Those boys will get you killed. We need to find Parker and Rosalie. They are after them. There is a hit out for you. Felix will come after you, your sister, and your brother. Until the debt is settled between Parker, Rosalie, and Felix. Please let me help you.

But that is not it either, River. Felix is not the only one after you and your family. Roman is also after you. Please let me help you and get you safe. Please tell me where your Mom and Dad are. You are not safe, your sister is not safe, and neither is your brother.

I also found a couple of tapes in there, along with a pic of a guy that my Mom is with. Not like just hanging out with, but shooting up heroin while having sex. I mean, there is a needle in my Mom's arm. This guy is not Roman, this is a different guy. I sort of remember this guy from when I was younger. I need to find out what I can about my Dad's past cases. I need to go through all those files till I find this guy. He is after me. I will find him. I will find out why.

I also reread the part about my sister and brother. My sister, I have never met. She is five now. I need to get her safe. But a brother. I need to find out about my brother. I didn't know I had a brother. Maybe I don't. Maybe it's another lie.

I go to the tape player I have and play the tape.

"No, Felix, I can't leave Roman." (My Mom)

"What about that other guy, Parker?" (Felix)

"What about him? He has the best drugs, even better than Roman's!" (My Mom)

"Baby, you need to leave them before you end up dead. We can run away together." (Felix)

"I can't leave you. But there is no way I can ever get out of being with Roman." (My Mom)

"What the fuck are you doing bitch!" (Unknown person)

Gunshots fired

"What the fuck you doing Roman that girl had nothing to do with any of this. Or anything for that matter." (My Mom screaming)

"I want you to know what I will be doing to you if you come here again. You're my bitch. Not his." (Unknown person now known as Roman)

Another gunshot

"Why did you just shoot him?" (My Mom screaming and

crying)

"He should have never slept with you. If you want to fuck with other dudes, then divorce me you whore." (Roman)

I hear someone get slapped.

"Don't you hurt the babies." (I hear my Mom scream!)

"I don't give a fuck about them babies or you. You're a bitch. And a whore. I am done fucking with you." (Roman)

I hear some more sounds like someone getting beaten up.

It's quiet for what seems like a lifetime, then I can hear sirens in the background.

"We need back up.. Two down with gunshot wounds and another one pregnant and barely breathing." (sounds like an EMT worker)

"Female gunshot victim. She has no pulse. Start compression."

"Male gunshot victim has a very faint pulse. You come to this one and take him to the Mercy. STAT!"

"Female pregnant victim beaten. We need oxygen over here. Barely breathing, barely a pulse. WE need to move her stat. Heartbeat of the fetus. Two beats are very weak. We need to move. NOW!"

Tape ends.

Why did they give this to me? What the heck is it? I am so confused. What is on the other tapes? What the heck is going on in my life? What kind of Mom did I have?

I am sitting in the chair in my room when Tatum walks in. He sees me crying and comes rushing over to me.

"Babe, are you OK?"

I can't even say anything. I just keep crying. I don't even know how to process all this information.

Tatum sees that I have a tape player in my hand. And a letter.

He picks up all the stuff. He looks at it. And the pic. I am not even sure if the pic with the guy is Felix because the tape said he was shot when I was still in my Mom's womb. At least that is what I am thinking. Me right? But they said two heartbeats. I just want to crawl into bed right now and never get out.

"Cain, Noah!" I hear Tatum yell. And then I hear both of them come running.

They see me crying and come running to me, but Tatum stops them.

"Look what she had."

They look at the stuff and take the tape recorder, and leave the room.

Noah returns with water and a root beer. I smile even though I am crying. I mean, I love root beer, and just the fact that he cares so much to bring me something to drink.

"Why don't you slip into PJ's, and we will turn on a movie."

I get up and go grab PJ's, and head to the bathroom. I come back out, and both Tatum and Noah are in bed with a space between them. I giggle and climb into bed.

"What do you want to watch?" I hear Tatum ask as he reaches the table next to him and grabs some popcorn.

I grab the remote and start to find something. Bring It On All or Nothing. That's what we are watching. I click on that movie because it is a movie that makes me smile. And right now, I need to be happy to wipe out all the confusion going on in my head.

"No, we are not watching this." I hear Tatum say.

"You know, River was a cheerleader in high school. Captain for four years."

He remembered. Aw, how sweet.

We watch the movie, and they stay cuddled up next to me. I

can't help but wonder about that tape. Right now, I don't think it is smart for me to leave this room. Maybe I just need to stay locked away forever. Maybe the guys were on to something when they told me no on the car. I do need a gun. I have a feeling I am going to need to start kicking some ass. And I will find both Felix and Roman and bring them down. I will save myself, and I will save my Mom.

24

Cain's Report

I start to listen to the tape after rewinding it and just about choke on my drink. Did I just hear someone get shot? Did they seriously beat up River's Mom?

I am scanning surveillance footage for this woman, and the pic is being scanned by Zeke. We need to find out who she is. And what connection does she have to Roman, and to Felix.

"Hello?" I pick up the phone.

"I have a hit on that pic," I hear Zeke say into the phone. "Her name is Misty Clark. It appears she has a connection to that Jackson guy who was at the Lounge."

"I have a tape here that needs to be analyzed. Make sure it is real. I am sending you a pic that was found in our, I mean, Rivers' stuff. Let me know who the guy is."

"I just got your email, and I don't need to run anything on who that guy is." Agent Parker has a file on this guy. His name is Felix, and the woman appears to be Rosalie, but this pic was taken about seven years ago or so. I didn't know Rosalie was back in contact with Felix. He was Roman's revival in the drug world. This means their location was compromised."

"That makes sense on how they knew when and where to follow River. I am so pissed right now."

"Dude, what is it with you three and this girl? I mean, she is hot and all, but you all are like in competition for her."

"Zeke, you will understand when you meet her. You can see the hurt in her eyes, but she is so feisty. I don't stand a chance with Tatum around. I mean, come on, we all know every girl likes a hot doctor."

I hear Zeke laughing. This makes me a little mad.

"Cain, you got the looks. You have that sweetness about you, too. But what are you going to do, date her? I mean, I know it's like every girl's fantasy to have more than one boyfriend, but are you willing to be one of her boyfriends?"

I had never looked at any of this this way. I mean, come on. We haven't been off to a great start. But I don't mind that she kissed Tatum or Noah. I just know when I kiss her, everything around me stops.

"Dude, we need to make her safe before we worry about being in a relationship with her," I say to Zeke. "Any ideas where Felix or Roman are currently located?"

"Sure, tell yourself that. Next thing you know, all four of you will be walking down one of the quick marriage chapels, all getting married, whose name are you going to take, Cain? We are working on locating them. We might have to go in and draw them out. I am thinking Jackson and this Misty chick are after her to collect the bounty that is out for River. I have found that there is talk about a large sum of money owed to both of them. Still figuring out what for."

"Thanks, Zeke. Keep us posted. Also, you've got to do some car shopping. Our girl wants a car, or a few."

"I like her already!"

I laugh and hang up the phone. I need to call Mr. Rizzo and report my updates and hit the hay. This girl is going to keep us on our toes, that is for sure. But I do like her, and I wonder how the others feel about her, too. I would be willing to date her and let them date her as well. But what will other people think about it?

I make my way back into the River's room and find them all sleeping. I grab my pillow and a blanket and lie at the foot of the bed, and fall asleep thinking about how I am going to keep my girl safe.

25

Training

A few days have passed since I got into a fight with the guys, found the tapes, and learned that my life is even more confusing than I had thought. I've been working out every day, actually a couple of times a day. I want to be ready, and I am not holding back. The guys say I could be better than them because of my tumbling skills, and of course, my jumps. They made fun of me because in one of the Bring It On movies, the girl says she is going to herkie the other girl in the throat. They said I could do that. Which made me laugh.

I was sitting in the hot tub when there was a knock at the door. I don't even bother to get out because anytime there is a knock, one of the guys gets it. I hear a new voice. A guys. I just stay put, figuring it is a hotel working, delivering something like food. I haven't been outside the hotel in several days.

"So you must be River." That strange voice said to me. I turned and looked to see where it was coming from. I see Cain walking out to where we are.

"Um, and who are you?"

"Hi, I am Zeke."

Zeke, the guy to take me car shopping. The guy Noah was talking to when we were on the bus. The mysterious Zeke. I checked him out. Nice body. Very toned. Nice looking. I would say another God. But I already have my hands full with these three. I am not sure if I could handle a fourth. Though the thought crosses my mind, I smirk at it.

"Nice to meet you, Zeke. Want to join me for a soak? I am not ready to get out. Trying to relax my muscles before working out again."

He chuckles. "Sure, we are just going to talk about what you want in a car today anyway. Then I will set up for you to test drive. And buy. Then train you to drive."

Train me to drive? What the hell is that supposed to mean? I already know how to drive. I have been driving since I was fourteen. Not legally till I was sixteen, but I had to learn young so I could rush Mom to the hospital or whatever else was needed.

I went to say something about that when I noticed he stripped down naked and climbed in. Um, hello, I am still sitting here. Oh my. Not that he needs to be ashamed of what he's got. But still. Does he not see me sitting here still?

I feel myself start to turn pink. Which makes him smile.

"I guess I should have warned you. I sit in here naked. I always do. And no offense, it won't stop just because you are here."

"None taken. But I have been driving since I was fourteen. I don't need training on how to drive." I am trying not to dwell on the fact that I have a naked hot guy sitting in the tub with me, and how hot it is making me.

He is full-on laughing at me now. I am not sure he should be laughing at me like that. This is making me mad. I just stare at him. That is not a way to impress me.

"Why are you laughing?"

"OH, that just cracked me up. I don't mean you need driver's training. I mean, you need to learn to drive. Do you know how to drive fast? Do you know how to outrun someone?"

"Well," I guess when he puts it that way, a little bit of training wouldn't hurt, right?

"Exactly. Now, what sort of car or cars do you want?"

"Hmm," I have been thinking about this, and I am still unsure. "I want speed. I want to be safe. I want to be able to get through anything."

"OK, how many cars are we talking about? Do you want any for play?"

"For play?"

"You know, go out to the mountains and play? Oh, I forgot you're from Michigan. It's not like you play there."

No, he didn't just say that, did he? "You know, just because I didn't have a mountain in my backyard doesn't mean I don't know what it's like to play. I have been down trails and to mud runs. I like to play and I like to get dirty."

I am really upset now. I think steam is coming out of my ears like in the cartoons when someone gets mad.

"You like to get dirty, huh?" He smiles at me. A smile that is jaw dropping sexy.

Seriously? Is he hitting on me? I am not sure what to take from this guy. But it makes me laugh.

"Yeah, I like to play in the mud like every girl back home. I have had a few mud wrestling competitions too."

Turn the being hit on to a turn down. Hopefully?

I was wrong.

"I like it when a girl can get dirty, and likes it. I would love to see you play in the mud. We should arrange it." He has that smirk again.

Face–palm

He laughs.

"Anyway, I will have a few cars to look at in a day or two. I will make some calls. I have a few different ones in mind. I can see you will be a fun one to shop with. We will head out to the range to drive. You can go fast there. Next business topic. I need you to pick out a gun."

Just then, Cain walks in with a few different guns. Um, OK. He walks over to me and tells me to sit on the edge of the hot tub and to dry off my hands and arms. I do, and they instruct me to pick them up and how to hold them. I do and I go through them to figure out which one I would like best. I want something that fits well and is not too heavy. I want a girly gun, but one with power.

After picking up and feeling the guns, I pick out one.

"Ah, nice choice, River." I turned and saw a smile on Zeke's face.

"I have a question; can I get it in pink?" This made both guys laugh.

Cain leans over and kisses me on my forehead. "Yes, princess, you can have it in pink."

"You picked out a Springfield XD .40. Pink will look awesome on that gun. Jazmine and Macky will come and take you to the range most likely tomorrow and shoot the gun. I will have your gun here in a day or two."

"You will have my gun here?" I look at Zeke.

He laughs again. "Yes, I will have your gun delivered here for you. Your grandpa will order it and have it delivered, I should say, in a few days."

"Why can't I go pick it up, you know, at a gun shop?"

"Because we always order our guns from the same person, with the promise that we will only use them."

Hmm, this seems fishy to me. But whatever. I guess if Poppy was ordering it, then it was all good.

I sit here awkwardly, not sure what I should do or how I should act. I don't know this guy. And I feel a little bit uncomfortable around him.

He asks me if I want a drink. I told him I would take water. He climbs out of the hot tub, walks inside, and comes back out with two waters. He sits back down close to me.

"You know, River, you are a very beautiful girl."

Hearing those words makes me blush. I don't think I could handle having another guy flirting with me, or wanting to date me, or whatever these guys are doing.

Just then, he leans over like he is going to kiss me. Oh no, what do I do? He gets super close to me.

"You have these three morons' wandering around with their heads cut off. Please don't hurt them."

Huh? That confuses me.

"What do you mean?"

His forehead leans in and touches mine.

"I mean, they want you, all of them. They would do anything you want. Tell them to jump off the roof, they would. Tell them you want to flee the country, and they will sneak you out of the country. Every one of them. They are my best of friends and I don't want you to hurt them. Because, girl, look at you. You could hurt them. In many ways." He smirks when he says that. Is he being naughty? He is whispering this in my ear, and honestly, his breathing in my ear is turning me on, and I am getting a bit excited. "So please tell me, you will not hurt them.

I mean, I have to protect them because let's face it, you have them being dumb to the world right now."

"I have no plans of hurting them. I really like them. They have grown on me. Even on days I want to punch them because they seem too controlling, I don't think I would be OK if they weren't around."

I can't believe I just told this guy this because I have yet to say it to any of the guys.

"Good, now I have to get going. It was nice meeting you, River, and I will be seeing you soon." He reaches for my hand and places a kiss on it. Climbs out of the hot tub and dries off, and dresses. And just leaves like it was no big deal.

I'm left with my thoughts. I take a sip of my water and think about what Zeke just said. If he has noticed how the guys are around me and about me, has Poppy? Have they? I mean, how do they feel about the whole situation, about how their friends like me? Do any of them consider themselves my boyfriend? I mean, we have never actually talked about it, and I haven't taken time to think about it. How would I feel if they went on a date? I would be jealous as hell. So, if I were jealous, how can I expect them to be OK with me liking them all? It is so unfair. It also sounds like I am being selfish. Aren't I, though? I mean, I want to keep all three guys, but there is only one of me. How would they even feel about that? No guy in their right mind would be OK with that. Not to mention, now I've met this other hot guy who, just by whispering in my ear, has got me still turned on.

I was lost in thought when Tatum came in and told me it was time to work out. Ugh, I wasn't feeling like working out, but this would be the "lesson," not that I needed it. I climb out of the hot tub and head to get changed. I meet the guys in the workout area only to find it's just Tatum.

"Where are Noah and Cain?"

"They had to run somewhere really quickly. But we can get started."

"Where?"

He doesn't wait for me to be ready, and he swings at me with his gloves on. I duck out of the way.

"Hey, I'm not ready to go."

He smiles and swings again, "If you're getting attacked, you're not going to be ready for it."

This is true, and I roll on the floor to the other side and swing at him. We go back and forth swinging at each other, making contact and sometimes not.

After about an hour, I hear the door open and the other two guys walk in. I have sweat pouring off me. I was ready to shower, but I noticed they had pizza.

"Pizza!" I jump towards them, grab it, and take off.

They start laughing. They start to chase me. It was nice to be a bit relaxed. I end up in the living room and throw myself on the love seat, and open a box.

I start to eat, not even waiting for plates. Noah comes in with plates, and Cain has water bottles. I grabbed a couple of pieces of pizza and took a sip out of the water bottle. When I set the water bottle down, it was empty. The guys look at me and laugh. Tatum grabs me another one, and I take it and smile shyly at him. That workout got me hot and thirsty.

Just as I was about to drink some more, the TV lights up. Whoa, I didn't know that this TV could make calls too. I see Poppy on the screen.

"POPPY!" I yell at him.

"Pumpkin! How are you doing, sweetie? How about your

workouts and stuff?"

"She is done with self-defense training." Tatum turns his cheek to Poppy to show him the nice red and bruised spot on it. I start to blush because I just did that a few minutes ago.

Poppy starts laughing. He turns his eyes to me, and I am blushing.

"Now, pumpkin, that is a good thing. The only other person to get the upper hand on Tatum is Jazmine. You will be meeting her tomorrow to shoot the gun and make sure you like it. I have ordered you a bright pink one, and it will be delivered at the end of the week. I am very proud of my pumpkin."

This made me so happy that my Poppy is proud of me. I smile.

"You know, dear," I see Gramma, "Your Daddy would be proud of you, too. You are just like him, darling."

I feel proud to hear that, but I am also upset that my Dad doesn't get to see me like this. I mean, he does from up in Heaven, but not in person; he isn't here to hug me and tell me I am doing a good job.

I smile at Gramma. "Thanks, Gramma, that means a lot to me. Please excuse me. I have to go take a shower. I am still sweaty from beating up Tatum." I grin a cheesy grin, and Gramma laughs.

"Yes, dear, go shower. We love you."

"I love you guys too." I smile and excuse myself from the living room and go shower. I figured they wanted to talk to the guys without me, and I definitely did need to shower.

After I showered, I got on and called AnnaB. I see her face, and she is getting settled in her dorm. She had to go early for some summer classes and cheerleading. We talked for a while about how she is doing. And how she's glad to be out of the hick town and in the city. She has been chatting to some guy for the last few days. I know it's not very long, but who am I to judge? I was just happy to see her face. I didn't tell her about everything that is going on. All I know is that I have to fix it before she comes this December because I don't want her life in danger, too. I tell her goodnight.

I call my Grandma and find out that Mom is still in rehab. Which is good news because she typically leaves after her seventy-two hours, and we are past that now. So maybe there is hope for her after all. I tell Grandma about learning self-defense and how I am learning how to shoot a gun. She told me she was super proud of me and that Papi would be too. I wanted to ask if I had a brother, but didn't think now was the time to do so. And I wanted to do more research to see if that was even true. I told Grandma good night and that I loved her.

I climbed into bed, surprised I hadn't seen any of the guys. I decided to watch TV and just put it on a channel. I must have fallen asleep at some point.

I woke up the next morning with Tatum next to me and no sign of Cain or Noah. Hmm, that is weird. I get up and go to get some coffee and to see if the other guys are out in the living room. I walk into the kitchen, and I can hear someone talking. I grab my coffee and head to the living room.

I am shocked to see two females sitting on the couch.

"Hi, you must be River." One of the girls said.

"Um, yeah, and who are you?"

The first girl is not very tall, but not super short either, has deep red hair, like chocolate-covered cherries or something. Or maybe burgundy. Very pretty, bright blue eyes, and her hair flows down to just past her shoulders. Beautiful smile. She reaches out to shake my hand or something. She walks closer to me and hugs me. "I am Jazmine. And this is Macky, or Mykayla."

She had longer, dark hair, both girls were fit-looking. Mykayla has brown eyes and, like Jazmine, she has a very beautiful smile. I find myself blushing when I see them because let's face it, I am not a model but both of these girls could be. I guess Vegas not only has gods, they have goddesses too. And I happen to be in the presence of two.

Macky says hi to me, and I say hi back.

"So go get dressed in something comfy so we can go shoot some guns." I see Jazmine smiling at me as she says it.

I nod and take a look at what they are wearing. Shorts and t-shirts. Nothing too fancy. I notice they are both wearing cowboy boots. Um, I don't have any with me, I couldn't fit them in my suitcase, and I never bought a pair.

"I don't have my cowboy boots. I left them back in Michigan."

Both Jazmine and Mykayla turned with their jaws dropped.

"Go get dressed." Jazmine shoos me away.

I run to the bathroom and brush my teeth. I'm going to get clothes. I found a pair of jean shorts that sort of look like the girls. I put on a pink T-shirt. I pull up my hair into a high ponytail. This makes me smile because it's like cheer hair. I grab a pair of tennis shoes and go to leave the bathroom when I run right into Tatum.

"I'm sorry."

"Are you in a hurry?" He smiles and bends down and kisses me. Deep and passionate. I love the way his lips feel on my lips. He traces my lower lip with his tongue and bites it a little. I feel my body temperature rising when he does it.

While he was kissing me, I heard a cough. He stops and turns around, "Jazmine, I didn't know you were here." He smiles at her and walks on out.

"Here." She hands me a pair of cowboy boots.

My eyes go wide. "Whose are these?"

She smiles. "Yours. We already knew you needed them and went ahead and bought them for you. Now come on. We girls are ready to have some fun."

She grabs my arm and we meet Macky at the door. She leads me out to a big Chevy pickup truck. Lifted, it is huge. I am so jealous. I think I need one of these in Pink instead of Black. I climb in and we take off out of town. Jazmine has the music blasting. I like this girl. She reminds me of how things were back home.

"So, have you shot a gun?" Jazmine asks me.

"Once a long time ago. I never had time with school, cheer practice, and taking care of my Mom. Oh, and working."

"It's cool, Macky and I are the best shooters. I think we can outshoot the guys any day."

This makes me smile. After all, I want to be better than them because I am sick of them thinking I am helpless. I am the only one who is going to get my Mom's life back, and my own. Plus, I have siblings I have to find and save too.

Jazmine pulls into this range thing. I see some targets on the far end of a field. She climbs out and gets out several gun cases. She sets them down on the table, and Macky yells at me to come on. I get out and walk over to her.

Jazmine shows me how to put together and take apart the gun. After we practice a few times, she shows me how to load and unload it. Where the safety is all that stuff. When she feels confident that I know all about it she tells me to load it and go shoot it. They each grab their guns and walk over with me showing me how to do it.

After I was steadily hitting the bull's eye, they added moving targets to the course and had me work on that. I think we spent several hours shooting.

"Well, I have to say I am impressed," Jazmine says to me.

"Me too." I hear Macky agrees.

This makes me smile and blush. I have never really impressed anyone; I mean, that isn't family. I have never impressed my Mom. She has never cared like I care about her.

"Come on, let's go get some food," Macky says to me, and loads up the guns into the truck.

Jazmine drives us to a little diner that has burgers and fries. We go in and order food, and we get some root beer floats.

"So, do you guys have boyfriends?" I thought I would find out what their relationship with the boys is. I don't need to step on any toes.

"Yes, we both do. Macky here is dating this super hot guy. His name is Rafael. I am dating a guy whose name is Nick."

"Her boyfriend is a model." I hear Macky say.

"Oh My Goddess, you're dating a model?" I am jealous, not that my guys couldn't pass as models. But I want to meet a real-life model.

"Yeah, but we don't brag about it. I mean, I am so busy and so is he."

We eat our food and continue with small talk. Macky lives in the hotel room with me, but she doesn't stay there. If that makes sense, since she comes home once in a while, she is always at Rafael's house. She told me I can redecorate if I want to.

She told me that her room just has a few of her clothes in there and that the guys can store their belongings in there. Such as clothes and stuff, and they already know they are allowed to sleep in there. Now that I know maybe once in a while I can have my bed, or I can sneak in there and sleep in Macky's bed if they piss me off.

"So are you dating either of the guys, or do you like them? I saw you, um, kissing Tatum. Is he like your boyfriend?" I hear Jazmine hinting at trying to get some dirt.

"I don't know. I like him, but I like Noah and Cain too. This sounds so weird. Is it weird that I like all three of them? I think Zeke is cute, too. But I don't want to hurt them." I sigh, "I mean, isn't it weird to really like three guys, can someone even like three guys or four at the same time?"

They nod their heads. "You know it's not weird. I mean, if you're not sure, date them all." I hear Mykayla say. "But Zeke is off limits. His girlfriend doesn't like to have competition. I mean, unless you're willing to date her too."

I just about spit out my drink when she said that. "Seriously?"

They burst out laughing. "No, she's not into girls, but she might not like you liking him," Jazmine says. "You will meet her in due time."

We finish eating and head back to the hotel. They walk me in and tell me they have things to do, and leave after Macky grabs a few things from her room. I tell them thank you and head to my room to change into PJ's.

That's odd, I don't hear anyone here. I walk around. There isn't anyone here.

I found a note on the bed.

*We didn't know when you would be home. Someone will be there tonight sometime soon. Lock the door. Don't open it for anyone. *

I went and locked it and sent them all a text message.

Text: I am back and heading to bed. Doors are all locked, along with the windows.

I climb into bed, turn on the TV, and get some sleep. I am exhausted after that long day of shooting the guns and spending time with the girls. I can't wait till I can go shopping with them.

In a day or two, I will have my gun and some new cars. Next on the list are Felix and Roman.

Then I will find out the truth about my brother and sister and save my Mom and my family.

26

A Plan

A few weeks have passed by now, and I have still been going to the range to work on shooting and spending time with Jazmine and Macky. Sometimes with both of them, sometimes with just one or the other. I still have been working out and doing self-defense stuff as well. I ordered a couple of different cars. I wanted some special stuff done to them so they didn't have any in stock. I have been out driving, and I have to say it is fun to drive fast. In the next day or two, I will have my actual car, or I should say cars. I have also been spending time with the guys. I am falling for them hard, and I still am not sure how I feel about being with all of them. It doesn't seem to be normal.

I am thinking about this while I am in the shower. Doesn't it seem selfish to want to be with all of them? I mean, I am kind of stringing them all along for a ride, and yet, I will still have to pick one. Maybe I should just cut the ties now before I get my heart or theirs broken. I mean, it's not fair to them. I haven't talked to them about this because I have been so worried about saving my Mom, sister, and apparently a brother. I am still unsure if I have a brother. Or of anything anymore. I reach up and grab a towel for my hair, and still let the hot water run down my back. It feels so good. I hear the music I turned on still playing.

Not really sure how to feel about it

Something in the way you move

Makes me feel like I can't live without you

It takes me all the way

I want you to stay

I am singing the lyrics as I shut off the water and grab my towel.

"AAAAHHHHH. What the hell!" I scream.

I hear chuckles. But I do not look very happy, I am sure.

"Hey girl, thought you would like to go drive your car," Zeke says to me.

"YAY! But don't you ever come in here while I am in the shower again. I don't think Shannon would like that all that well." Shannon is his girlfriend. She is a very beautiful blonde girl about my height, and she has long legs. Beautiful like Jazmine and Mykayla.

He starts to laugh again. "How is it fair that those losers get to see you but I don't?"

"Hey, those guys are not losers. I happen to like them."

He gets this funny smirk on his face. "Oh, you happen to be in 'like' with these guys out there. I happen to think you have more than a little bit of feelings for them, like I WANT them."

This made me blush. I mean, how do I respond to that? I do like them; I think I have stronger feelings than just liking them. But I don't want to hurt them. I mean, does this even make any sense?

"What I feel about them is between me and them. I don't know if I should talk about this with you."

I mean, should he know how I feel before the guys do? Or before I know how they feel about me?

He chuckles. "Come on, get some clothes on, I have something for you."

"What?"

"Just get dressed. I'll wait in the living room."

"Um, OK?"

He turns and leaves. "Just wear something comfortable. And well, movable."

"Huh?"

Too late, he was already gone. I run to the bedroom and grab some clothes. Confused on what to wear, I just grabbed jean shorts and a t-shirt along with tennis shoes. I pull my hair up off my shoulders, as it has been hot here. I brush my teeth and head out. I find Zeke sitting with Cain and Noah.

"Where's Tatum?"

Cain laughs, "He had to go to work for a while, he will be around later." He stands up and heads over to me and kisses me. Slaps me on my butt. "Have fun!"

I turn to say something to him when he leaves the room. Just as Noah kisses me. "I'll see you later." He leaves, and Zeke is standing there with his hand out.

"Are you ready?" Zeke asks me.

"Are you going to tell me what I should be ready for?" Still blushing from the attention I am getting.

"Nope, just come with me."

I grab my purse and go to leave when Cain hands me some French toast sticks to eat on the go, and I tell him Thanks.

I rode with Zeke for a little while, and I noticed we were heading to where we had been driving. I think to myself about how exciting this is. I have been loving the fact that I can drive fast out here. I have been learning so many things on how to swerve around things, in and out of traffic, and that stuff. How to lose people in small places, and so many other things. I am surprisingly good at it. I give all the guys a good run for their money.

We pull into the driving range. I see my Hennessey Venom GT all black sitting there. I don't even wait for Zeke to stop; he slows down, and I jump out. I ran over to my baby. I have a huge ear-to-ear grin on my face as I walk around her. I open her up and notice the interior is hot pink, just like I wanted. I am super excited. I had to have her custom-made because we could not get pink as the interior. That is why I had to wait to get my car.

I turn to grab my keys just as Zeke snaps a pic and sends it as a text message.

"What the hay, dude?" I ask him.

"Ah, I was told to take a pic of you with your baby. And that grin on your face, I couldn't pass that up."

I couldn't be mad. "You better send it to me!"

Just then, I got several pings on my phone. I see messages from everyone, even Poppy.

"You don't have time right now. It's time for both of us to be on track. And we are also going to include Macky."

I have yet to have more than one person on the track with me.

"I am going to be on your side and we are going to talk through these," Macky says to me and hands me an earpiece. I put it in my ear. She checks them to make sure we work and I can hear her.

"I will be following you. You two have to trust each other to get out of this. I will follow you, River, and Macky drives like you. She will be your go-to person. Now I know you have trust with the guys because Tatum guided you to safety when you got kidnapped, but right now you have to trust us to get you to safety. So now you have to rely on Macky and your gut. Got it? If you make it back here with more than two minutes between us, then you made it safely. We only need two minutes to set up the trap for these people. OK? Did you get it?"

I nod my head and take my keys. I start her up and take her for a quick drive so I can feel how she handles. When I make it back, I only find Zeke there. He comes to the window and instructs me that Macky is now in this range somewhere. Mind you, this is like a huge ass city out here. It has buildings, roads, alleys, the whole kit and caboodle. He told me to wait five minutes so he could go hide, then I was to take off. Go anywhere I wanted, and he would find me. When I see him, I am to do what I was trained to do. He walks away, and I watch him get in his car. I check the time. I breathe in and out, and I remember that I have to do this for my Mom, for my sister, for my brother (I mean, if I have one right?), and most importantly, I have to do it for me!

After five minutes, I take a deep breath and exhale. I take off. I go several different ways, and after about ten minutes of driving. I look up and see Zeke's car behind me.

"Macky, I have someone following me," I inform Macky.

Over the next twenty minutes, she instructs me to turn in different ways. It doesn't lose him, which I had already known it wasn't going to. I had to get out of the city and go fast. She instructed me to take a long road, and I floored it. Zeke had a hard time keeping up with me when Macky instructed me to turn one way, which was a way I wasn't familiar with, but I remember I had to rely on them. I did. And I was going down areas I hadn't been down yet. Following her lead, I saw another car, but it wasn't the one that Macky had driven. I still listen to what she tells me to do.

After the high speeds, with now two cars behind me. I picked up another car behind Zeke. I was instructed to do more turns and ended up with Zeke several minutes behind me after the turns I was instructed to make. I finally made it back to the start and looked at my clock.

I wait for Zeke.

Just as the first car pulls up behind me, both Jazmine and Noah jump out and lay the tack strips. Jump back in and take off. I pulled up out of view of Zeke's car, and after about five minutes, he and the other car came. He ran over the strip and was then boxed in by the others.

I jumped out of my car and was surprised to see Tatum and Cain. I ran over because I couldn't believe they took out Zeke's tires like that. I get hugged by Noah first, and then down the line with the guys. As soon as they set me down, another door opens. I turn and see my Poppy.

"POPPY!!!!!" I scream and run over to him.

He picks me up and twirls me.

"Pumpkin. I like your new ride."

"Thanks, Poppy. I do too. She drives so nicely."

"I could tell."

Just as he said that, another car pulled up with two guys. One gets out and goes to my car.

"I don't think so. That is my car." I swing at him, thinking he is trying to steal my car. He ducked. But doesn't say anything.

"Pumpkin, he is taking the car to where we need it. Now come on with me, we need to go back home and talk. Gramma is waiting there to see you, too."

I climb into Jazmine's car with Poppy and Macky, and the guys all climb into Tatum's car, and we head back.

"Pumpkin, I am so impressed with your driving. I have not seen anyone drive like that since...."

I stare at him. Since when?

Oh, it hits me. "Since Daddy?"

"Yeah, pumpkin. You drive just like him. There is so much about you that is like him. It is all good, of course. You are just like him. I can see that same look he had in his eyes in yours."

"Your Dad was a legend." I see Jazmine looking at me in the mirror. "Everyone wants to be like him."

This made me smile. At least I know my Dad was important and was very respected.

"Thanks, Poppy, and thanks, Jazmine. I know my Dad was a great man. It makes me proud to know that I have some of those same qualities he has." I say to them, I can feel my eyes water, and then an arm goes around me. I look and see Macky holding me.

We drive the rest of the way in silence.

When we get back home, I run in and hug Gramma. I excuse myself to go change. I want to be in some sweatpants or something different, and I need to freshen up, too.

I am in my room listening to some music, throwing on some different clothes, when Gramma walks in.

"Hi, Gramma."

"Oh, dear. How are you doing?"

"I don't know Gramma." I feel the need to just say what I want to say.

"What don't you know about?"

I knew she wanted me to share what I was thinking or feeling. Right now, I need to get it off my chest to someone.

"Well, first off. I like those three guys. I think I like, like them. Not just a little bit, but a lot a bit. I mean, if that even makes any sense. I don't know how they feel. I feel like it is selfish to be kissing them, I mean, kissing all of them. They have all seen me kiss the others, they don't seem to mind. But is that fair? There is only one of me, and there are three of them. How can I expect them to be with only me when there are three of them? I am so confused about how I feel about them. And secondly, I want to find these monsters that are after my Mom, brother and sister, and me. I want to make them pay. I want my life. I want to have my own life, not live in fear. I want to know where my sister is. And I want to know if I have a brother. And if I do, where is he? I want to know they are safe and that my Mom is safe." I start crying because really, this is way too much for someone my age. I am so young. Yet I have so much on my plate.

My Gramma hugs me. "Oh, dear. Your Mom is safe. And I have to say I am so impressed with her. She is getting better. She is still in rehab."

Hearing this makes me smile. This is the first time she has ever been in rehab for this long. Maybe she is trying to get her life together.

"Also, don't you think you should talk to the guys about how you feel? I mean, from what I can see, I see three guys who are falling head over heels for you. They don't care that you kiss their friend. Why should you beat yourself up over this? Why can't you let them make choices for themselves? I mean, from the sounds of this, you are not even giving them the chance to tell you what they want or how they feel. And why can't you have three boyfriends? I mean, if a guy did it, it would be OK. People wouldn't even bat an eye, so why can't you do it?"

Gramma makes a point. How can I choose if I am not willing to first talk to them about all of this? They have a right to tell me how they feel about all of it. But am I ready to face this? The truth is, I want to save myself first. I don't want to drag them down if something bad is going to happen to me. I would rather spare them from getting hurt. Isn't that what good people do?

Gramma looks at me, "Have some fun while you're still young. You only live once, and you might as well have some stories to tell your grandchildren, right?"

This makes me laugh.

"So what stories do you have to tell me?"

It is now her turn to laugh. "Trust me, darling, you don't want to hear the stories of when I was undercover. Yes, your Gramma was undercover and did some pretty wild things. My, my, my. That is all I am at liberty to tell you. But I can say, three guys are nothing."

My jaw must have hit the floor.

She starts to laugh. "It was before Poppy and I got serious."

She gets up and walks out of the room. I am still too stunned to move. I just sit there staring at the door.

"Hey, River, are you OK?" I see Jazmine walk in. I think I stunned her because she was just staring at me.

"Um, I think I am. I can't believe what my Gramma just told me is all."

"Oh," she says, "Your Poppy wants to talk to all of us. And he said to come get you because he wants you in there too."

Hmm, that seems weird.

"OK, I will be out in a second."

I get up and finish changing. And turn off my music. When I turn around, I am the only one left in the room.

I sent AnnaB a text about what Gramma said to me. I had to

share it with someone.

When I got to the living room, the only spot to sit was between Tatum and Cain. I sit down, and Noah sits between my legs on the floor. I started to play with his hair. He has such soft hair. I like the way it feels between my fingers.

"So, we have located this Misty chick that wants to talk to River."

I turn my focus to Poppy. She could be a key to finding out about Felix or Roman. I want to find her.

"Yes, sir, we have," Zeke says to Poppy.

"Where?" I so rudely ask. I didn't care if it was rude, but I want to know. I want to go get that bitch. I mean, she has already messed with my head. I am not going to let her mess with my family.

"Calm down, River, or I will ask you to leave," Poppy says to me. Truthfully this pisses me off.

"You will not talk about me, and what I am going to do without me. You either include me or I will leave." Didn't I tell them this once already?

"Like I said, calm down. We need to take steps to catch them and to keep everyone safe. Getting too much power in the head will cause you to get kidnapped, again."

UGH, this makes me so mad I want to blow up. I just want to help.

"Fine," I say and cross my arms.

Just then, Tatum and Cain both take my hands, making me uncross them. I want to yank them out of their hands just to pout some more. But I have to say I like the way my hands fit in theirs and how they feel.

Jazmine turns to us, "She has been going to a club on Friday nights for the last three weeks. We are thinking of picking her up on Friday and starting to get some answers."

"So we are going to walk into a club and grab her?" I ask. This didn't seem logical. How can you snatch someone from a club?

Wait, that happened to me, didn't it?

"Not exactly," Macky says.

"This is why we've been training you. She wants you, not us. She knows us and won't talk to us. So you girls are going to go to the club. You are going to get her to follow you out of the club, because she will want that bounty money. You will get her to follow you out of town to the building where you and Mr. Rizzo had dinner. And we will trap her there, and then we can question her." Zeke says to me.

"No, that isn't happening," Cain says. At the same time, Noah is shaking his head, and I can feel Tatum getting tense.

"It is the only way we are going to be able to get her," Zeke says again. Jazmine is nodding her head.

I haven't had time to speak yet.

"No, we are not risking her safety. We will find a different way to do this." Noah says this time.

"There is no fucking way I am letting her put herself in harm's way because you are an idiot and can't figure out a way to get this dumb cunt." This was Tatum.

I was shocked at their reactions. And it made me feel so good to know they didn't want me hurt.

"Stop! I have been training. You all have been helping me. If you can do it, I can do it. This is one of my biggest battles, and I have to help. Not for myself but for my family. I need to save my Mom, my brother, and my sister. I need to find out if I have a brother. I need to find my sister. You guys can help me, stand beside me, and encourage me. Or you're just a roadblock in the way, and I will do this without you. I don't need your permission, but I trust you. I trust you more than anything else, and I want you to help me with this. I know you will keep me safe, so help me do this. Or you can get up and leave now, and I will do it without you." I was so mad that once again, the boys were thinking I was just a child. Or at least that is how I was feeling.

I see them debating with their demons or whatever, inside. I glance at Poppy, who seems to be amused by all of this.

"Fine, we will do it your way. But our way too. You have to promise that if it gets too dangerous, you will bail and let us do something different." Tatum speaks up.

"Dude, do you think we would let her in harm's way?" Zeke asks Tatum.

"Not intentionally."

Jazmine shakes her head. "So the plan is we will go to the club, us three of us. Have some drinks. Or whatever. Do some flirting. When we get her attention, we will watch her. I don't think she will approach us all together. Maybe you are by yourself in the bathroom, but we will never leave you for very long. We want her to follow you out. Macky and I will get in a different car. You will get your baby. We are hoping she will follow you. But we want you to keep her behind you. If she gets extras, we will instruct you on what to do to lose them or bring them. Either way, we want you to get her to the old diner. Go in, leave the door open, and go out of the tunnel. One of the guys will close the door." Jazmine takes a big breath, and "We will question her and then figure out what to do with her."

What to do with her? "You mean take her to jail, right?"

Macky was the one to speak up. "Sometimes it's better to follow them. They will lead us to their boss. Like Felix."

I was getting it now.

"Sounds like a plan to me," I say with a smirk.

"Does to me too." I see Poppy smiling. I am still unsure how I feel about this, but I am glad to know that soon we will have this chick and I can start to get answers. Little do they know I will not be leaving through the tunnel. I want to know the answer too, and I have a feeling they wouldn't tell me everything.

I want to help; I want to do this. I know I can do this. I have been trained, and I have Dad on my side. RIP Daddy.

27

Club

The next day, I get to go shopping, which is awesome. Jazmine, Macky, Zeke's girlfriend Shannon, and I all go to the mall.

"So, River, have you ever been to a club before?" Shannon says to me as we get out of Jazmine's truck.

"Does teen night count?"

I hear laughs. "I keep forgetting you're from hick town."

What the hell is that supposed to mean?

"Ummm, hick town? Or are you meaning to say Michigan?"

Jazmine smirks, "Yeah, that's what we meant."

"Just because I am from Michigan doesn't mean I don't know how to have fun. I haven't been eighteen that long, and we don't have clubs for under twenty-one in Michigan, well, not anywhere I know. Other than teen night. That is twenty and under. I have been to a couple of them, but I would rather just go have a beer at a house party."

I am a tad bit pissed. Just because I have grown up poor and didn't have all this where I was doesn't mean I was sheltered. Does it?

"You're right. We are sorry. We didn't mean it like that."

Shannon gives me a hug that ends up turning into a group hug.

Jazmine grabs my hand and pulls me into a dress shop. "You will need a drop-dead gorgeous dress that will drop jaws."

Drop jaws? Only three jaws I want to drop. This makes me smile, and I start dreaming about them staring at me and their jaws dropping. I can picture it already. I want to see this. I want to see it in person. I have to find a dress that will do this. Hmm. This is an upscale dance club. Something I have never in a million years thought I would go to. And here right now, I am buying a dress to go. What kind of dress would I need, or want?

Browsing racks, the four of us start shopping.

Tons of dresses. Long ones, short ones, puffy ones, skin-tight ones, every type of dress you can think of. I am thinking about what would be the best type of dress for the club. I want to dance, but I want to look grown-up too. I see some cute dresses and grab them.

"Um, no." Macky and Jazmine both say to me at the same time.

I turn around. I didn't even know they were standing there. "What?"

"Those say, how do I say it without being rude, high school homecoming. Not really club material." I hear Shannon say. She wasn't even near us, so how did she know what I had in my hand?

"Here," she tossed me a dress. If you could call it that. It looked more like a shirt to me.

I was staring at it when the other girls started to laugh.

"How about we try on some of the dresses you like, and then try on some we think you should wear, because they are more club style," Jazmine says to me and smiles.

I think about what she just said. I guess that is a good idea.

These dresses I picked up do sort of look like high school homecoming. But I have always wanted to try on and wear dresses like these when I was in high school, and could never afford them. Which kind of made me depressed, thinking I had all this money waiting for me, why couldn't it have been around when I was doing things like this back then?

I nod my head and head to the dressing room, and so do the others. They have arms full of dresses. We spent the next couple of hours trying on dresses. I try on dresses that I would have loved to have in high school. Even some prom-style dresses that I knew I couldn't wear in the club because they were way too long.

The four of us laughed and had a ton of fun. I haven't had this much fun in a long time. I don't even think I have had this much with AnnaB.

Which made me think of her. I needed to text her.

Text to AnnaB:

Hey girl, I miss you. How are you? How is cheer practice at that big college of yours? How's the guy friend? I am attaching a pic of me trying on some dresses. I am going to the club on Friday. Tell me what you think.

I attached a picture, then several more of different dresses.

Text back from AnnaB:

OMG... My girl is finally living a little... I went out to a couple of different clubs with some of the cheerleaders here. None that required me to dress up. Add that to our must-do list. Who are you going with? The hot gods? Or are you going to play the field a little bit and venture out on your own? Anyway, those dresses are so high school. But you do look hot in them. Try something for the adventurous River. Live a little. Skin tight, and short. You will be able to dance better. Trust me. Send me a pic of what you decide. <3

I text her back to tell her I am going with the girls. I hadn't told her about them, but she tells me she is glad I have some female influences in my life since she can't be here.

I think I want to cry. I don't know if I can do this. Right now, I want to run away. I am not sure if I am strong enough to handle all of this. I feel some tears roll down my cheeks just as Jazmine walks in with some new dresses.

"I am sorry, I just walked in. Are you OK, River?" She sits down next to me and wraps her arm around me.

I try to stay strong, but this girl has this overpowering way to make me want to tell her everything.

"I don't know if I can do this. I don't just mean the part of going and getting this girl. I just mean all of this. I didn't want this life. What kind of life did my parents bring me into? I miss my Dad. But I hardly had him in my life as much as he was working. My Mom was so hooked on drugs that she couldn't even see me graduate from high school. She had to hand over my baby sister because of the drugs. Neither she nor my sister's Dad could stop using it long enough to keep her. Now a drug lord is after me because who knows? I just want to disappear. I want to be someone else. I struggled all my life to make sure I could eat and that my Mom was taken care of. I had to get a job so I could do things like cheerleading and going to dances. And yet, I had all this money sitting there waiting for me. Every day, it seems like another lie about who I am comes to the surface. I just don't know how much more I can take from this. Who is River? Because right now I have no idea who River is!"

Jazmine holds me, and I can feel her rubbing my back to soothe me. "You know, River is a girl who is one of the strongest people I know. She had a great Dad who loved her very much.

He would have done anything to make her smile. She has grandparents who would do anything in this world to make her safe and happy. The River I have grown to know would do anything to find out the truth of who she is and what happened in her parents' past. This River I have grown to respect would never let someone stand in her way. Or to allow someone she didn't know to bring her down. I know you can do this. If I didn't believe you could, I would tell you. But this is the only way you will know the truth. I want to help you, but if you're not ready. I understand, and we can wait. I will back up your choice one hundred and fifty percent. I will always have your back. You need to do this for you, River, not anyone else. Not for your Mom or sister. Not for the brother you may have, but let's get these pricks so you can be free."

I sat there thinking about what she had just said to me. I know she is right, but can I be that strong? Can I do this for myself? I have only really been thinking about my family and not letting them down. But most importantly, I can't let myself down. I have to do it for myself. Me and me only. I want to be free. I want to be free of the burden of my Mom. I want to be free of what could have been. I want to know the truth. Who am I really? Do I have a brother? I have to do this.

I hugged Jazmine. Well, I gave her a great big bear hug and squeezed her so tight her eyes might pop out. Well, not really, but it felt like I was squeezing her that hard.

"Thanks, Jazmine. You're right. I do need to do this for myself. I need to know the truth of who I am, not for any other reason, but I want to be free of this. I don't want to carry my Mom's mistakes around forever. I want them gone, and I can't do it on my own. I need your help. I need everyone's help."

She smiles. "That is the spirit. Now, try on some dresses that are made to dance in the club. Let's find the new you. You want to be."

I take a couple of dresses she brought in and try the first one on. Not something I would wear typically, but it's cute. It is sparkly, super short and my boobs are about out of the dress. I laugh at myself. Not the dress for me, but it's not bad. I walk out of the room, and the girls start doing cat calls. It makes me blush and laugh at the same time.

"This is cute, but not my style. Got anything else?"

I see all three of them shake their heads yes and shoo me back to the dressing room. They had already found their dresses, and I was the only one left. I think I spent the next ten hours trying on dresses until we found the perfect one.

Macky got a black short leather-looking dress. Reminds me of a biker outfit, but it's a sexy short dress. Shannon got a white short dress with the top part that crossed over top of her boobs. Hers is open a little bit at the boobs. The two of them look smoking in their dresses. Jazmine bought two. One with a long sleeve and no sleeve is dark blue with some sparkly designs on it. Her second one is a short light blue dress that ties around the neck. Not sure which one she is planning on wearing, but she had to have both. I like the dark blue one best. I decided to be super daring. I mean, I am young, and I only live once. I bought a short dress. The black skirt part looks like it's leather. The top part is bright red. Ties around the neck and has a black built- in belt that is just under my boobs. I even bought thigh-high black leather boots to make it complete. The girls said it was the one that would have all of Vegas drooling over me.

Not that I wanted all of Vegas to drool over me. I only want my guys, too. I wanted them to get tongue-tied when they saw me in this. And this outfit, I know, will do it.

We stop by the pretzel place at the mall and get one. We sit at a table and make small talk while we eat, and then continue our journey. We buy accessories. And just have some plain, good old-fashioned fun.

When we get back home, Zeke grabs up Shannon and kisses her. He turns to tell us goodnight and takes off. As he walks out the door, two guys are standing there. I was a bit nervous, but he wasn't. Come to find out they are Rafael and Nick. Let me tell you, my god, more hot guys. I can see why Nick is a model. Super sexy smile, tall, nice tan, and is super cute. Rafael looks like he just walked off a movie set. Dark skin, that sexy smile that has you wondering the meaning behind it. It is very naughty. He is tall as well. The girls hug me and take off. And honestly, if they were mine, I would be taking off too. I smirk to myself. I can hear Gramma and Poppy laughing in the other room.

I walk into the living room and sit down.

"Did you have any fun, pumpkin?"

"Yeah, I really did."

"What did you buy?" I see them both looking at me.

I take out the dress and boots and show them.

"That will look great on you, dear. And think of all the fun you will have." Gramma says to me with this huge grin on her face. I see Poppy shaking his head, but he doesn't say anything. I smile to myself.

"I think I need a shower and head to bed. Have you seen or heard from my guys, I mean from the guys?"

"Tatum said he would be over later, I think. Or maybe it was Cain. Or Noah, or maybe they all said they would stop by." Gramma smiles at me while she says that. I can see Poppy has a confused look on his face.

Great, they can't even take a decent phone message or a personal message for me. I think to myself as I walk into my room.

I hear Gramma and Poppy laughing again.

I can only think, oh goodness. I don't even know what to know. I jump into the shower while listening to tunes. I shower and allow the water to run down my back. I love the way the hot water runs all over my body. While the water is running down my back and all over my body, I start thinking about the future and what is going to happen. All that I can see is my guys. Not one but all three of them. I want them and need them in my life. I can't see myself without them. I only want them. But how do I tell them that I like them? Not just one of them but all of them.

I was so lost in thought when I felt my hands touch me. I jump.

Tatum laughs. "It feels like forever since I have seen you."

It hasn't been that long. I mean, I just saw them all yesterday. None of them stayed last night, but it was because I spent the rest of the night with Gramma and Poppy.

He grabs me and pulls me into his naked body. He leans down and kisses my lips as he pulls me up, and I wrap my legs around him. He keeps kissing me deeply, like he just can't get enough of me. I can't get enough of him. I kiss him back deeply and have my tongue running along his lips. I lean my head back a little bit and kiss up his neck to his earlobe. I nibble on it. I hear him moan. It makes me moist, not just moist, I am wet. I want him so bad. I kiss my way back to his lips. And start to kiss him deeply. I want him so bad. I know he wants me too. He pushes me up against the wall of the shower. I wrap my fingers in his hair. He started to kiss down my neck and made it to my nipple and ran his tongue around it and started to suck on it.

Just as he was letting it go, we heard a cough. We both turn and look to find Gramma standing there, smirking.

Tatum lets go of me, and I place my feet on the ground, and we shut off the water. Her smirk is still plastered across her face. I am not sure if I should smile or what. Tatum grabs a towel and gives it to me, and gets himself one too. He kisses me, wraps the towel around himself, and leaves.

"Gramma, what the heck?" I am unsure of what to even begin to think about this.

"Now, Darling, I was young once. And he is, well, you know."

I am sure my face is now a bright red color like a fire engine.

"Why did you walk in on us?"

"Oh, yeah. Poppy wants to talk to you and Tatum." She turns and leaves the room, leaving me standing there.

I am so embarrassed by that. I run and get dressed in some PJ's and a t-shirt and head out to the living room. There I find Poppy, Tatum, and Noah. Gramma is missing. I look around and don't seem to find her. I walk in and sit down next to Noah.

"Now, pumpkin, this is the layout of the club. I want you to be familiar with it. Just in case. This is what we have planned. You girls will go to the club. Misty will show up. Make sure she sees you. If you see her go to the bathroom, make sure you go in. Give her time to start a conversation with you. If you're gone too long, Jazmine or Macky will come "bump" into you in the restroom," he says, using the quotation fingers for bump as he was talking. "Get her together and follow you after the club. When you leave, your new baby will be outside, parked. Watch for her to get in her car. We will have it near the car she shows up in. Make sure she follows you to the diner where we had dinner. Watch your mirrors and listen to Zeke on your earpiece. Jazmine and Macky will be in one car, Tatum and Noah in another. Cain and I will be waiting at the diner. If someone else follows, you need to tell Zeke. He will lead you and tell you what to do. When you get there, come in casually, getting her to follow you in. When she comes, we will trap her and question her. You will leave through the tunnel, and Zeke will guide you through your earpiece. Gramma will be here when you return. So do you understand?"

I nod, knowing that is not the plan. But I do not want them to know I have a different plan in mind. I still have to figure out what I am planning, but for now, I will make them think I am going to do what they want. I have to do this. I know deep down she will not tell them anything. I mean, she wants to talk to me, why would she? I yawn, making it seem like I want to head to bed.

"Are you tired of pumpkin?"

"Yeah, Poppy, I am. I think I will let you boys finish, and I will be calling it a night. Shopping wore me out."

They laugh, and I hug Poppy and both boys lightly kiss me. I leave the room and head to the kitchen for a bottle of water. When I sneak back out, I listen to them for a second.

"So, I see that you both have been kissing my granddaughter. I am wondering what that is all about. And are you intending on hurting her?" I can't believe Poppy just asked that question.

Tatum is the first to speak. "Honestly, sir, I truly care for your granddaughter. I don't want to pressure her into anything, but I would do anything for her. Even if she asked me to disobey you and take her far away. I would in a heartbeat. I know Cain and Noah both feel the same way. I care for my friends; we have become more like brothers over the years."

"I don't mind if she kisses them, I don't mind if they go out.

I know it's not normal. But our whole lives are not normal. And with her being in danger, I don't see how any of us can have a normal life. I will always be next to her, and if I can't be, I would be happier knowing that it is one of them that is. We just aren't so sure how she feels. Or even if she would be with any of us, or all of us. We mean no disrespect at all towards you, her, or even Mrs. Rizzo." I hear Noah say.

My heart skips a beat. Hearing them say this.

"And Cain, he feels the same way?"

"Yes, sir, he does." They respond to him together.

"I see." I hear Poppy saying. "What about sex? How are the three of you going to feel knowing she is having sex, or already is having sex with someone else?"

My jaw drops. Did Poppy ask that?!

"Sir, I don't know how Noah and Cain feel, but if she wants to have sex with me and one of them, I would rather know she is having sex with them and not some guy she picks up at a club, bar, or online. I trust my friends, and I trust her. I truly, deeply care about her. And from what I know, they do too."

"Honey, you know that this is normal. Well, maybe not normal, but for us it's normal. And they are young. Let them be. Your granddaughter is so happy. If three guys make her happy, at least she picked three of the best agents our company has when it comes to young, successful agents. Plus, they respect her, and care for her, and worry about it, and they would do anything for her. Isn't that what you want for her? I would go as far as to say that they are beyond just liking her dear, I would say that they love her."

Gramma's words made my mouth drop, and I headed straight to my room. I need to not hear anything else for the time being. I need to sleep. I need to talk to the guys and see how they feel, and see if they were saying that just because Poppy had their backs up against a wall.

I switch on the TV and lie in the middle of the bed. I fell asleep.

The next morning, I found two arms around me. One from Tatum, the other from Noah. No Cain. And it makes me a little sad. I kiss both their foreheads and go and work out. I need to make sure I am in shape. And I need to think. I have so much on my mind, I am not even sure what to do, or what to think. I need AnnaB.

Text to AnnaB:

So, I found a dress. Now I have to meet some crazy lady and get her to follow me so I can catch the person who is after my family. My Poppy wants me to get her to this diner and then leave, but this girl doesn't want to speak to anyone but me. AnnaB IDK what to do. HELP!!!

Text from AnnaB:

Then you need to talk to her. Do whatever it takes, but talk to her, girl. How do you get her to the diner? How do you leave the diner? Can you change it there? Can you talk to her at the club?

I think about what she asks me.

Text back to AnnaB:

I got it. I am going to lock this girl in the diner and lock out the rest of them. Cain and Poppy will be on the inside, but I will be behind the door and shut it and lock her in when she walks in. I will then question her. I just want my life back. I love you, AnnaB.

AnnaB back to me:

I love you too. Text me when it's all done. Sending prayers.

Over the next few days, no one talks about the plan. It's like everyone knows about it, but it becomes real if anyone says anything about it. My guys have been busy doing work and other stuff, so on Thursday night, when they want to take me out, it's a real big surprise.

They take me to this old warehouse. We walk in, and my mouth drops.

"Um," my eyes wide open and my jaw on the ground, that is all I can say.

Tatum laughs, "So Mrs. Rizzo said that when you were little, you and your Dad played Candy Land all the time. She said that every night your Dad would challenge you to a game, and every night you would win. I know you're scared about tomorrow night, and it is a lot to take in. So, we decided to play Candy Land, adult style."

I am looking around the warehouse. It is a life-sized Candy Land board. Every piece of the board was laid out and made out of candy. Bridges made out of skittles, candy canes, and gingerbread houses the size of forts kids would build in the backyard. Giant marshmallows and even gumdrop land. Each square is made out of a starburst. They even made the little people from the board, too. It is so much to take in.

"So, we are the pieces of the game. Wanna play?" Noah looks at me, waiting for me to respond.

All I want to do is eat the board. I shake my head yes, and my smile is ear to ear.

We spent the next few hours playing Candy Land and eating the board. Taking turns drawing cards and moving up the road of Starburst. I can't stop smiling. And I have to say that the whole time we have been playing, I haven't even thought about tomorrow one bit. Until just now.

We head home after we are done, and all three guys climb into bed, and I climb into a free spot. It felt so nice to have them all there with me. I need to have them all with me. It is so comforting knowing they are there for me. They made me a life-size Candy Land game. Who does that? Duh, my guys do. It reminded me of playing when I was younger with my Dad. I really miss him.

Dad, I know you are in Heaven looking down at me. I need your strength. I need your knowledge and your support. I need you. I need you to guide me tomorrow, and let me know that I am making the right choice in not following the plan. I really, really need to know what is going on, Daddy. Please help me.

I close my eyes and attempt to go to sleep. Which, mind you, is a very difficult task tomorrow. I toss and turn all night long. I did get some sleep, but not as much as I would have liked.

I smell bacon. MMMM. I love bacon. I roll over to find that all the guys are still in bed with me. Awe! But, if they are here, who is making bacon? I try to sneak out of bed, but I am grabbed by Noah.

"Where are you going, Wonder Woman?"

I laugh quietly. "To get bacon, duh." I can't believe he just asked me that question. I mean, for real, it's bacon.

He smiles. He pulled me close to him and lightly pressed his lips on mine. Very softly kisses me. Then he runs his tongue on my lower lip and begins to bite on it. I let out a soft moan. And kiss his lips a little harder than he had been kissing me. I love the way his lips feel on mine. I forgot that the other two are on the other side of me. It's like at this moment, it is only Noah and I lying here, lost in the passion of this kiss.

I let go of his lip. "I want bacon." I smile and climb over him to get out of bed. I feel him shift under me and climb out after I do.

"I want bacon, too." His saying that makes me giggle.

He wraps his hand in mine and we head out to get breakfast. We made it to the dining room. "Ewe." We hear.

"Jazmine!" Noah says rather loudly.

She burst out laughing. "Hi, big brother."

Brother? Did I know that Jazmine and Noah were brother and sister? Um, this just got weird.

He just kept looking at her, like he was scared to say anything to her. It was a very awkward moment.

"Hey Jazmine, did you make bacon?" I decided I would break the silence.

"Yes, I did. You need to eat well today. So you can be ready for tonight." She looks at Noah's hand inside mine. "I've got some last-minute stuff to do. And I will be having lunch with Nick. I will be back to head out to the club later. You two love birds have fun."

And with that, she left.

"OK, I didn't know Jazmine was your sister. But I guess there are still a lot of things I don't know."

Noah pulls me for a kiss, nothing too hot and steamy, but enough of a kiss to let me know that he wants me and wants to be with me. I can feel my body relax.

I spend the day just relaxing with the guys and Gramma and Poppy. It was nice to just hang out like a family. And Poppy and Gramma are so much fun. It was what I needed to get my courage up for tonight.

Text to AnnaB:

It's the big night. I am ready. I love you and will text you later. <3

I know it's time to get ready. Poppy and the guys, and don't forget Zeke, are going over all their details on what to do. Zeke will stay here with eyes on us via his laptop. I guess there are some cameras in place at the club. He will be watching us and talking to the guys if they need to come in. Cain and Poppy are to head out in a little while, but Cain will be dropping off my car near where Misty is parked. He will text me where it is. You know they are going over all those details.

I head to my room and jump in the shower. I was expecting one of the guys to join me, but this is how business goes.

I get out and put a towel around me. I get out my bra and panties I picked out for tonight, and slip them on. I work on my makeup and my hair when Gramma walks in.

"How are you doing, dear?"

"Anxious and a bit nervous. Gramma, are you still an agent?"

"Yes, dear, sometimes I still do stuff. But I am not actively involved with it like I used to be." She looks at me, confused.

"Can I ask you a question?"

"Besides that one?"

I laugh, "Yeah."

"Shot."

"If your gut told you to do something but others don't think you should, or keep telling you that you can't do it. Would you just do it? I mean, if it keeps eating at you, that something isn't right, and you are the only one to fix it, but no one agrees on what you do?"

"Interesting. Sometimes, even teammates or other agents don't always see the bigger picture. Good agents sometimes have to take risks and make quick decisions to get the responses they need or to solve a case. The Rizzo family is known to take risks and venture on their own. Sometimes you have to take hold of your life and do what is best for you." She smiles at me. And her response is like she knows what I am talking about. "I love you, dear. And I trust you."

She kisses my head and walks out of the bathroom.

Thanks, Daddy

I put on my outfit and boots just in time to hear Macky, Jazmine, and Shannon come into the bedroom.

"OH. MY. GOD." All three say in unison.

"Is it bad?"

Heads shake no.

"Ready?"

"Group photo," Jazmine takes out her phone, and we take a selfie. And head out to the living room.

I am stopped by three hot, amazing guys, Nick, Rafael, and Zeke. Poppy is shaking his head no, like he wants me to go back into the bedroom and never come out.

I look at Noah, Cain, and Tatum. They can't stop staring at me. Their jaws are on the ground. And they are even shaking their heads no. Zeke has a smirk on his face, but he walks to Shannon and kisses her. Nick does the same, and so does Rafael. They walk out to the door.

"I think we made a mistake." Tatum looks at the rest of them, and they agree with him.

"I don't think so. Now you can kiss me, or I am leaving without one."

I get a kiss from each of them, and Poppy reminds me of the plan. The guys tell me again that they think this is a huge mistake. But I don't agree and leave with the girls.

We get to the club and make our way in. We ordered some drinks. Music is blaring. I love this place. I get my drink, and I want to dance. I grab Macky and head to the dance floor. Sugar by Maroon 5 is playing, and I am singing it while dancing.

I spotted her. That woman who was following me when I went shopping.

"She's here. We need to move closer so she sees me."

Macky nods, and we move closer to the floor here.

She makes eye contact with me. When she does, she leaves the dance floor and heads to the bathroom. I leave and head that way about thirty seconds after her.

"No, she's here now. I have to follow her. Jackson, I got this. Yeah, I will call you when she leaves."

I hear her talking on the phone from the door before I enter the bathroom. I make my way in and bump into her.

"I am so sorry, I didn't mean to bump into you."

Misty looks at me, "It's alright." I can see she forces a smile on her face.

I go to a stall and text Zeke.

Text: *She's here. And she called Jackson. She is working with him.*

I flush and come out of the stall, and she is still in there.

"Do I know you?" I ask her.

"You need to save yourself. They will not stop till you're dead. I have more tapes for you."

I was shocked. "What?"

"Listen, just leave Vegas." She leaves the restroom.

I dry my hands and head back out. I told Jazmine what she said. I can see Misty watching me. I continue to have a few more drinks. If you were watching me, you would think I was getting drunk, but my drinks are virgin. I dance some more, and before I know it, several hours have passed right on by. I got my text from Cain, and I went to leave. I tell the girls by and Shannon gets in her car, and Macky and Jazmine get into theirs.

I climb into my car and start it up. Turn on some music. And wait for Misty to get in hers. About a minute later, I see her on the phone again, walking in front of my car, and she sees me. She climbs into the car two down from me.

Show time.

I told Zeke via earpiece I was leaving and heading out of town. She was on the phone again, only I assume that it was with Jackson. He tells me which way to go, which is clear right now.

I turn up the song playing. It's me right now. I start singing the lyrics.

Oh, it's just me, myself and I
Solo ride until I die
'Cause I got me for life (Got me for life, yeah)
Oh I don't need a hand to hold
Even when the night is cold
I got that fire in my soul
I don't need anything to get me through the night
Except the beat that's in my heart
Yeah, it's keeping me alive (Keeps me alive)
I don't need anything to make me satisfied (You know)
'Cause the music fills me good, and it gets me every time

I am just driving and looking in my mirror. No extra cars. So far, so good. She keeps following me. I can feel my nerves kicking in.

I pull into the diner and park close to the building. I can hear her car not far off. I go in and hide behind the door. I can vaguely hear Cain and Poppy talking, I think to Zeke. They are expecting me to come into the office and wait.

I hear the car door shut outside, and Misty is on the phone again. "Yeah, at that old diner. She just went in. I will grab her and bring her to you."

I hear the footsteps drawing closer, and Jazmine's truck is getting closer. I can hear it off in the distance. Come on, Misty,

I need you inside before Jazmine gets here. I have to lock her out.

Just as Misty walks in and gets through the door. She turns on a flashlight and walks far enough ahead of me that I get the door locked up before she even knows. Under my dress, I pull out my gun. I walked up to her.

"Now, you're going to do exactly what I say, and no one will get hurt."

Misty jumps and turns to face me, and I have my gun pointed at her. Her hands go up.

"You need to put that gun away. I am not going to hurt you, River. I said I want you to leave to save yourself."

"That's nice, but I need some answers first. So why don't you hand me your phone and purse and have a seat at that table?" I can now hear Jazmine and Macky trying to get in. I know that any minute, Poppy and Cain would be coming out, and I want Misty not to see them. She has to face away from the office so they can only see me.

She hands me her stuff and has a seat at the table. I tie her to the chair so she can't overtake me. I sat down across from her.

"What do you want with me? Why do you keep following me?"

Just as I finish that question, I see Poppy and Cain run out of the office and stop. They are just staring at me.

"I am following you because I have too. Jackson was hired by someone to either kidnap you or kill you. There is a huge debt owed, and you're the one they are trying to collect it from."

"Keep going, tell me everything you know."

"That's all I know." She lies to me. I can tell she is lying by the way she doesn't look me in the eye. I have to show her I am serious. I slap her across the face, and her eyes get huge.

"I can't believe you just hit me. That isn't you. What have you done to River?"

"Bitch, you don't know River. River wants her life back. I have been lied to for way too long, and I will do that again. And again. Or maybe I should just shoot you and forget about you."

"OK, OK, no need for that. Jackson, I think, was hired by Felix. Felix and Roman have teamed up to get your Mom. She took a lot of drugs from them. Half a million dollars' worth. From each of them. They want her, they want their money, or they want her children. You have a twin brother; they are after you, too, but they wanted you first. They feel you will get a point across because your Dad is the reason for all of this, and they know he has money. I swear that is all I know. There is a debt, and you are the "prize," so to speak. So tell me where your Mom is so she can settle this."

"No, how do I get hold of Felix or Roman?"

"I don't know. Look in the trunk of my car. There is a box of stuff I took from Jackson. Dirt he has on them. See, your bounty is only a quarter of a million. Jackson wants more. He found this stuff to sweeten the deal. Take it. I will tell Jackson I lost you here, and you will never see me again. I will jump on the next flight to LAX."

I stare at her. I hear Zeke in my earpiece. He told me I was one crazy girl and that Misty was telling the truth about the stuff in the trunk.

"I want Jackson to give me a way to get hold of Felix or Roman." I handed her the phone.

After a few minutes of her staring at me. I get up and walk over to her. "Now. I want you to have him arrange a meeting."

"Jackson, call Felix. I got her. Let me know when and where to bring her."

She hands me the phone. "He will text when he is done with the arrangement."

I grab the phone, and next thing I know, I feel a sharp pain, and then a really weird pain. I start to get dizzy and don't know what's going on. I can hear Poppy yelling my name, but I can't answer him. I see Cain running over to me. And catching me before I fall on the ground. I can see his face, but I can't hear him. I don't know what's going on. His face is spinning, and then everything goes black. I hear the muffling of what sounds like gunfire or cannons, and I feel someone running with me.

Did I just die? Because I was not expecting Heaven to be so dark. I was expecting to see light. That is what I have always been told, anyway.

28

The Boys Reports

Cain

I walk out of the office to see my girl with a gun pointed at Misty. I couldn't be more proud, scared, and confused than I am right now. Mr. Rizzo and I stand back and allow her to work.

My jaw just about hits the ground when I see her slap Misty. I can't believe what I was watching. Completely unaware of what is going on around us.

I stand in awe when, all of a sudden, I feel Mr. Rizzo yank me and find some big guy standing behind us with some sort of gun. I find Tatum fighting him, and the gun goes off.

"NO!" is all I can hear everyone say. I turn and see a look on River's face. It is a look of pain, and what the hell is going on? I can't believe it. She has been hit with something. I have to get to her. I don't even care what is going on right now. I have to save my angel. My beautiful angel. Nothing else at this moment matters but her. My brave, strong angel. I take off running for her, but the look on her face is blank. I grab her before she hits the ground.

Just as I grab her, the doors burst down. I see Jazmine, Noah, Macky and Tatum with Mr. Rizzo beating the shit out of all different kinds of people, and people with guns. I scoop up River and take off out the side door and to her car. I have to get her out of there.

"Zeke, we need backup. We need some help. They found us. I repeat, they found us. Rivers has been shot. I had to leave."

"Cain, breathe. You need to breathe. Get her the hell out of there. I already am on my way. Not that far out. Get her back to Mrs. Rizzo. Stat."

I am so freaked out, I don't even know how I managed to start the car.

"Breath, Cain." I keep hearing Zeke in my earpiece. I mean, this is not the first time we've been in a fight, but this is the first time that my girl has been hurt. I have to save her.

Cain, pull yourself together. Come on. I have to focus. I take off and head as fast as I can back home. I can't get there fast enough.

"Cain, dear. I already have the medical bag waiting. You can do this, dear. I know you can." Those soothing words convince me that everything is going to be OK. I know that Mrs. Rizzo is ready and already knows what is going on. "The rest of the gang has everything under control, too."

It's funny that she has tried not to be an agent for so many years, yet she always seems to get caught up in our mess. It makes me smile.

I pull into the hotel and stop right by the door. It seems Mrs. Rizzo already had help waiting for me, doors opened, car taken care of, I just have to get her to the room. I rush into the open door and run her to the living room on the couch.

"Go, Cain, go get some water. I need a few minutes. You do

too. You need water, she would want you to calm down."

"I can't, Mrs. Rizzo. Is she breathing? I can't leave, I have to stay right here." I am pacing, which I know is driving Mrs. Rizzo batty, but I can't leave her. I just can't do it.

I see her searching River's body, and I can see her chest moving up and down. She is still breathing, and that calms me down. I slow my pacing. And watch Mrs. Rizzo. I am very confused about what she is doing.

"You say she was shot?"

I look her in the eye and shake my head yes.

"Help me find the bullet wound and get her out of this outfit and into something more suitable. Go get her night shirt."

I run to the room and find her long nightshirt. I rush back out to find that Mrs. Rizzo doesn't have a bullet, but a dart of some sort. As I walk closer, the dart is a syringe of some sort. I grab a baggie out of the medical bag, and she places it inside.

"Where was that?"

Mrs. Rizzo grabs some bandages and places them over the spot that had been in. "Her hip." She sighs. "Zeke, I have a syringe for you to test. I need to know what was in it."

I am finally able to focus on my earpiece.

"OK, Mrs. Rizzo. We are on our way back. Cleaned up the diner. No one else is hurt. How is she?"

I hear the concern in Zeke's voice.

"Dude, until we know what the fuck was in that. We don't know how she is. Currently, she is passed out but breathing." I was annoyed that he asked that. How the fuck was she supposed to be? We don't even know if what she was shot with is going to kill her.

"Sorry, dude. I wasn't even thinking."

I went and took some medicine for my headache and drank

water. By the time I was done with that, everyone else showed up.

I picked River up and took her into her room and laid her on the bed. We can watch her on the camera we have in there on the computer screen, but we need to go over what the heck happened.

I don't want anything to happen to her. I think I am falling in love with her.

I take that back; I don't think, I am.

Tatum

I don't even know how that guy got in there. I could see him, and he had a gun, and no one else knew he was there.

I had just snuck in through the tunnel. Even though Mr. Rizzo had told us that River had everything under control, and to stand guard just in case. I wanted to see it with my own eyes. I needed to know she was OK. When I went in there, he had that gun pointed at her.

I jumped on him, and the dude fell into Mr. Rizzo, who, in turn, grabbed Cain. I was throwing punches and wrestling around with this big dude, trying to get the gun away from him. Just when it went off.

"NO!" Everyone was yelling.

OH! MY! GOD! I will never forget that look on River's face. It was the most awful look ever. I was screaming. The pain in her eyes. It was unbearable. They went all glossy. It looked like they had iced over.

I could feel and see Cain running to her, and this big dude took that Moment to overpower me and flip me over on my back, throwing punches. But honestly, I didn't care; I just needed to make sure River got out of there.

Cain grabbed her, and just then, the doors burst open with several other people.

"Zeke, dude, we need you. Help. River was shot." I scream into my mic.

"Tatum, I'm already on my way. Cain gets River out of there."

"Cain, can you hear me, dude?"

Oh hell no, something better has not happened to Cain, too. I turn just in time to see him skate out the door.

"Zeke, he is outside. Keep talking to him."

A few minutes pass. I am punching the fuck out of this dude. I need to get the fuck out of here. My girl is hurt. I am a doctor. I need to take care of her.

"Zeke, we need backup. We need some help. They found us. I repeat, they found us. Rivers has been shot. I had to leave." I hear Cain saying to Zeke.

"Cain, breathe. You need to breathe. Get her the hell out of there. I already am on my way. Not that far out. Get her back to Mrs. Rizzo. Stat." Zeke will calm Cain down enough to her the fuck out of here.

I knock the dude out and feel a punch to my head. I turn around and swing. I think there are like fifty dudes in here. Misty is still tied up. Mr. Rizzo ties up the big dude and is creeping around while we knock them out.

I can't believe Jazmine and Macky are even beating up these dudes. Hell Yeah.

I hear Mrs. Rizzo talking in my earpiece. "Cain, dear. I already have the medical bag waiting. You can do this, dear. I know you can." Those soothing words convince me, so I know they had to convince Cain, too. "The rest of the gang has everything under control, too."

I don't know for sure if we got it under control, but I wasn't going to tell Cain that. He needed to be there with River. I need to know she is going to be OK.

After all the guys are tied up. We turn around to talk to Misty. And get to the bottom of this.

"What the fuck?"

She was gone. How the hell did that happen? Her cell phone lay on the ground next to the chair. But no, Misty. All this for nothing? Seriously?

We gather up all the cell phones from the guys and the personal information they have. We take pics of their IDs. Load the assholes up in a car and drive down the road and leave them.

I need to get back to the hotel. I need to kiss River. I need to hold her. I need to see her.

It was the longest ride back to the hotel.

I walked in just in time to see Cain taking her to bed. I follow him. I need to see her. He doesn't say anything to me, lays her down. I kiss her forehead and see that she is breathing, and leave Cain behind.

I walk out with a sigh of relief. I hugged Cain. I don't normally hug him, but I needed to right then. I mean, he did save our girl. Wow, I just said it, instead of saying my girl, I said OUR GIRL.

I feel a few tears on my cheeks. But I see I am not the only one with tears. I know what this means.

I am not the only one in love with her.

Noah

Where did Tatum go? He was just right here. Did I just see him go into the tunnel?

Mr. Rizzo had just told us to stand guard and that my girl was holding down the fort. He said she brought her gun. I couldn't be more proud of my girl. All grown up and holding her own. She even made up a plan on her own.

But why is Tatum going in there?

I'd better follow him so he doesn't get himself into trouble.

What the heck? I am not even inside, and I see Tatum swinging. So I took off running to him. What does that big dude have in his hand? Oh Hell No, it's a gun.

Just as I jump at him, I hear the gun go off. I look up just in time to see the bullet. Ummm, no, that is not a bullet, what is it? I see it going right towards River.

I yell loudly, "NO!!!" She looks up at me just as that thing hits her. Her eyes went wide, like, what the hell was that? I start to run towards her, but Cain is faster. I also feel something grab me. Well, not something, I should say someone.

I see River's eyes go all cold-looking, and they are twitching. It's like they are spinning, sort of like when you're having a seizure, but not nearly that bad. She is falling, but Cain gets her in time. Oh, thank goodness.

"Get her out of here," I yelled at him just as the door burst open. Who the hell are these people? I see Cain running out the side door and know I need to buy them time. And I need to get the hell out of here.

"Zeke, dude, we need you. Help. River was shot." I hear Tatum screaming.

"Tatum, I'm already on my way. Cain gets River out of there."

"Cain, can you hear me, dude?" Zeke repeats.

I have to stay focused on the task at hand. I don't have time. I can hear Zeke asking Cain over and over again if he is there.

I keep fighting these dudes. Throwing punches at their faces and knocking them down. I want to kill these dudes. Skip tracking them and hunting them down later. They could have killed River. I don't even know if she is OK. Honestly, she didn't look like she was even alive.

"Zeke, we need backup. We need some help. They found us. I repeat, they found us. Rivers has been shot. I had to leave." Oh, I love hearing Cain speak. Now, just to get him to my girl safely.

"Cain, breathe. You need to breathe. Get her the hell out of there, I'm already on my way. Not that far out. Get her back to Mrs. Rizzo. Stat." Zeke has a way to soothe anyone.

I can hear him telling Cain to keep breathing. Truthfully, hearing that makes me breathe. I have knocked out four or so dudes when I turn and see my sister is kicking the hell out of some dude. It's a good thing River wasn't the only cheerleader around here. Both Jazmine and Macky were high school cheerleaders. They both would have cheered in college if they hadn't been agents and chosen not to go to college right now.

I am tying up some dude. Just as I hear Mrs. Rizzo talking to Cain. It was so soothing to hear her say, "Cain, dear. I already have the medical bag waiting. You can do this, dear. I know you can. The rest of the gang has everything under control, too."

Not long after that, we have everyone tied up. Now to get answers from Misty.

What? Where did she go? How is that even possible? To escape all of us? Oh, goodness.

I pick up her phone and hand it to Zeke. He will need to figure stuff out for us. I take out all the phones from everyone's pocket. We take pics of their IDs and save them. Spend what seems like an eternity loading up all these dudes into a car. We park them at the park down the road and leave them to fend for themselves when they awaken.

I can't stop tapping my foot and I know it is bugging the piss out of Jazmine. But I just really can't stop. I do it whenever I am nervous.

"She's going to be an OK big brother," Jazmine says, trying to make me feel better. I love my little sister.

"I sure hope so. I don't know what I would do if she's not."

"You love her, don't you?"

I think about what she just asked me. Do I love her?

"It's OK, brother. Don't tell me before you tell her. But I think it's good for you. I really like her. And I am OK with her seeing all three of you, if you are."

I smile at that. Not many people would be OK with that sort of thing.

I walk into the hotel and make my way to River's room. I see Tatum kiss her forehead and head out. I can see her chest going up and down, so I know she is breathing. Why did this happen to the most beautiful Wonder Woman ever? I kiss her cheek and head back out. I see my best friends in a hug, and I walk over to them. I put my arm around them. One around each of them. I can see the tears in their eyes. This makes me cry, not that I wasn't going to cry, but they make me fall apart. I lose it when I see them.

I love her. I know I love her. But does she love me? Does she love any of us? I can tell by how my friends are acting that they are falling in love with her too. What do we do? When do we tell her? Do we tell her? I mean, she doesn't even talk to us about this. So what do we do?

But right now we need to get her better. We need to know she is going to be OK.

I see Zeke take the bag and start to leave. I ran over to him and hugged him.

"Thanks, Zeke."

"No problem, but I need to head to the lab so I can figure out what she was poisoned with so we can get her better."

"I know."

He turns and leaves. And Jazmine hugs me. She and Macky head to Macky's room and get settled for the night.

"Can I tell you guys something?" I ask Tatum and Cain.

"Anything," Tatum says, and Cain shakes his head in agreement.

"I love River." There, I just came out and said it. But I didn't know Mr. and Mrs. Rizzo were listening.

"Me too." Both Cain and Tatum speak at the same time.

We all look at each other. What do we do now?

"What do we do?" I want to know what they think.

"Tell her." I hear Mrs. Rizzo say, and we all turn and look at her. "I think she is scared that you three wouldn't go for it. But I have a feeling she likes you all. Well, I think she more than likes you three." She smiles. "Honey, let's head to our room, not much more we can do tonight till Zeke is done. Tatum, I am trusting her in your hands. Let me know if there is a change."

And just like that, they leave.

I think we need some sleep, and we all want to be near River. I climb onto her feet. I think Cain and Tatum need to be near her side more than I do. Tatum for medical reasons, and Cain just so he can settle himself down after all that crazy tonight.

I hold on to her foot while I fall asleep.

29

Sister?

Oh, my head hurts. Why do I feel like a truck ran over me? Man, it hurts to move. Where am I?

I open my eyes. OK, I am in my room. How did I get here? The last thing I remember is... Shit, Misty. I sit up fast. Bad idea. It hurts to move. How did I go from the diner to my bedroom? What the heck happened?

I look around the bedroom and don't see anyone. That is really weird. Normally, I would find one of my guys with me. But I am here all alone. How long have I been here?

I go to pick up my phone from the nightstand where I always leave it. And it's not there. OK, that is another weird thing. Where is my phone?

I rub my eyes and stretch. Throw the blankets back and get out of bed. I go to the bathroom and use it. Boy, my bladder was fuller than anything else ever in my life. I thought I was going to explode. I brush my teeth and head out to see where everyone else is.

I walk out and it's. Really quiet out there. I see Tatum sitting on the couch. Looks like he is reading a book. Hmm. I walk over and sit down on top of him.

"Hey, beautiful. How are you feeling?"

"Tired, sore, and I have had a bit of a headache. And honestly, it hurts to move. What happened?"

I see him on his phone. He must be texting everyone.

"Well, you were setting up a meeting when you got hit with a dart. The dart was a syringe filled with a general anesthesia that knocked you out."

"WHAT?" I think I am kind of yelling because it hurts my head. But I have a right to. I mean, once again, I am drugged. "How? I mean, how did it happen? Where is Misty? We need to get Jackson and Roman. Did you still go to the meeting? How long have I been out?"

"Some guy got in, and your grandpa and Cain didn't see him in there. He was about to shoot you when I jumped him. While we were fighting, the gun went off. It was a dart thingy syringe that ended up knocking you out. We were then attacked. Somehow, they knew we were there. Cain left with you while the rest of us were in a fighting match. Misty got away during that time. Zeke has been going through her phone to pull data to see what we can use. And you have been knocked out for about forty-eight hours." He leans over and kisses me.

I sit there and take all this in. I didn't say much and decided I needed to be alone. "I'm going to take a shower." I get up and don't even wait for Tatum to reply to me, and go take a shower.

I am not even mad that I was drugged, I am not even mad that I ended up in bed and have lost two days. I am so pissed that I did what I had to do and got that woman and we had her, and where is she now? We will probably never find her. I mean, if it were me, I would skip the country and never look back. Zeke better find some useful information, or all of this was for nothing. We aren't any closer than we were before. I was so angry that I started to cry. I cannot even believe this has happened.

I was crying so hard that I didn't even notice that the guys had come into the bathroom.

"River, can you hear us?"

What? I look up with tears flowing down my cheeks. But I cannot stop crying. I feel my body being lifted and hugged. I don't even know who has me, but I just keep on crying.

"I screwed up."

"No babe you didn't screw up."

"Wonder Woman, you did great."

"You were so wonderful. You were great in action, it was the best thing I have ever seen."

"I lost her. This is all my fault. I changed the plans and didn't tell anyone. I just want my life back."

I can hear them saying it will be OK, and that I didn't do anything wrong. But I know I did. And I will have to try and fix this. I want my Mom, sister, and brother to be safe.

I think I will end up falling asleep.

The next thing I remember is waking up in bed. I want to start crying again, but I know I need to talk to Poppy. But I need to shower.

I get into a hot shower, and it feels good running over my body. It makes me more relaxed. I was so zoned in letting the water run on me that I didn't hear the bathroom door open.

"Beautiful, how are you doing today?" I turn and see Cain standing there.

"I need to talk to Poppy. I am still sore, and I still want to cry. How did this all happen? How did I screw up?"

Cain wraps me up in a towel as he soothes me. "Princess, it's not your fault. Things happened, and you were awesome in there. I am so proud of you." He pulls my body into his as he hugs me. I can feel the tears slowly stop.

I pull away and go get dressed. I need to talk to Poppy. "Cain, where is my Poppy?"

"In the spare bedroom."

I walk out of my room and knock on the door to the spare room.

Gramma opens the door and has her suitcase behind her.

"Gramma, where are you going?"

She hugs me, "Dear I have to go home and take care of a couple things. I am so glad that you are finally awake. I want you to take it easy for a while. I am so proud of you dear. And your Daddy would be proud of you too." She kisses the forehead and goes to leave, I pull her into a big bear hug. She squeezes me. "I love you dear."

"I love you, too, Gramma. And thank you." I wave to her as she leaves.

I walk into the room and find a bed, several desks with computers on them, and a couch. I look at everything. I see Zeke and Poppy in there talking. They haven't noticed me yet.

I hear Poppy, who seems to be upset right now, yelling into his phone, while he and Zeke talk. I can't hear what is being said, but he has an angry tone. I walk further into the room and I catch something.

"NO! THIS IS MY GRANDDAUGHTER YOU'RE TALKING ABOUT. YOU WILL FIND OUT WHO DID THIS OR ELSE. I HAVE HAD ENOUGH OF THESE GAMES. SHE HAS PROVEN HERSELF AND WENT OUT ON A LIMB. WHICH IS MORE THAN I CAN SAY FOR YOU. SHE IS JUST LIKE HER DAD, WHO ALSO TOOK RISKS AND ENDED UP BEING THE BEST AGENT WE HAVE SEEN. NOW

FIND OUT WHO THOSE MEN WERE."

"Poppy," I quietly said, not to draw too much attention.

Zeke and Poppy both turn to me.

"I've got to go, but this conversation isn't over. I expect results when I call back." Poppy hangs up the phone, and Zeke gets up so I can sit by him. He hands me water and walks over to the desk and starts typing, and pulls stuff up.

"Pumpkin, how are you feeling?" He gets up, hugs me, and kisses the top of my head.

"I'm sore and feel like a truck ran over me. But other than that, I am mad, and angry, and upset." I can feel my eyes start to fill up with threats of tears to pour over.

"Talk to Poppy."

"How could we just let her go? How could I be so stupid to change the plan? I should have followed your orders. I messed up, and this is all my fault."

"Pumpkin, first off, it is not your fault. Second off, she got away because we were all being attacked, and she was there one second and gone the next. Your plan worked, we got information, and we are working on our next move right now. It was by far your fault that this happened. It was ours. Cain and I were so stunned that you just took over like that. And so damn impressed that we couldn't help but watch you. Which we don't typically do, and we let our guard down. Some guy we are assuming came in through the tunnel, was about to shoot you when Tatum jumped him. We never saw it coming, but if the guys had been more focused outside like the girls were, he may not have gotten in, or if Cain and I had been paying attention, he would have never made it out of the office. Now go over there to Zeke, he has some stuff to show you."

I get up and go to Zeke, still processing the stuff Poppy just said. I sit down and look at the computer.

"What is this?"

I am staring at what appears to be text messages.

"These are text messages between Jackson and Misty. Now we have a number to trace for Jackson. We have found a location for him. We plan on taking him after we do some surveillance at his house, so we know our plan of attack. We have already pulled blueprints for his house and know the layout. We also think Misty is lying low for now."

"What are you waiting for? Let's go on a stakeout."

Zeke and Poppy laugh.

"What?"

"Pumpkin, it's already being done. Both Tatum and Noah are there, and so are Jazmine and Mykayla. They are taking turns taking pictures and watching for different things. They should be back around dinner time, and Cain and Zeke will take over."

"I want to help."

"We know you do, that is why I am showing you some more stuff on here. I need you to start doing some searches on the leads we have for your brother and sister. We are still not positive if you have a brother, but we have been doing some searches and found that you may have one. So, I need to keep checking these leads."

"Why can't I go with Cain and you do this?"

"Because the doctor said you can't do anything like that for the rest of the week. You have to follow doctors' orders."

How dare he do that to me? I will have to say something to him later. But I will work on this in the meantime. I want to find my brother and sister so much. I want to make sure they are OK and safe. I would do anything for that.

I hear my stomach growl and look up, and both Poppy and

Zeke are staring at me.

"Come on, let's get you some food." Zeke grabs my hand and we head to the dining room.

When we walk in, there is food already on the table. Bacon, fresh fruit, eggs, biscuits, and gravy. I am so hungry that I sit down and dig in.

"Cain, did you make this food?" I yell into the kitchen.

He walks out with juice to drink and walks over and kisses my head. "Just for you, I did. But I guess Zeke can eat too."

I laugh and we eat in the quiet.

As we finish up, the boys start talking about taking a nap before the big night they have in store for them. I clean up the mess so they can lie down. I go back into Poppy's room and find him asleep too.

I sent a text to my Grandma telling her I am OK. But I want to talk to her, so I go outside and call her. I think we talked for about an hour, catching up, and I told her all about what had happened. She told me that Gramma has been keeping in touch, so she knew everything, and that she is glad that I am doing OK. She told me Mom is still in rehab. That she still has a few more months in there. Which is a relief to me because I know she is safe there. I tell her I love her, and I hang up the phone.

"WHAT DO YOU MEAN YOU DIDN'T CALL?" Oh, no Gramma is mad. She doesn't usually get mad.

"I mean, I didn't call them. I have no idea what you're talking about. Calm down, dear, we will get to the bottom of this."

"DON'T YOU DARE TELL ME TO CALM DOWN. I HAVE BEEN

KEEPING MY COOL WHILE THESE PRICKS PLAY THEIR GAMES WITH MY FAMILY. IT IS TIME TO STOP THEIR GAME PLAYING. I COULD HAVE ENDED UP IN A TRAP IF I HADN'T CALLED FOR A LIMO TO BE WAITING FOR ME. THANK GOODNESS THE PILOT TOLD ME THE PLANS AHEAD OF TIME."

"Noah, call the pilot, and you and Tatum go get his phone. We need to trace that call. Honey, I know you're mad, but you need to calm down."

"Sono così incazzato ora sono circa a pugni qualcuno." (I am so pissed right now I am about to punch someone). I have no idea what she just said, but I can tell she is so mad.

I hear a ding on the computer. That is weird. I walk over to it, and I see an instant message pop up.

I look at it.

MESSAGE:

I have the information you requested.

What information, and who is this for?.

MESSAGE BACK:

Well?

MESSAGE TO ME:

We have to meet. I have papers to give you. Meet in our spot. Midnight.

I walk out of the room. I still hear Gramma yelling in Italian. She sees me and walks over and smiles and hugs me. "Gramma is a little upset right now, dear. I think I am going to go sit outside and get some fresh air."

I smile and nod in agreement. Poppy turned towards me.

"Poppy, someone sent a message and wants to meet at midnight tonight."

He looked up in surprise. Ran to the bedroom, and I followed.

"Pumpkin, this might be the key we need." He smiles.

"The key to what?"

"Finding your sister." He walks over and kisses the top of my head. "Go get dressed. You are coming with me."

I run to my room and find some jean shorts to slip on and a t- shirt. It is really warm even at night here that I would want to be comfortable. We take off and drive for about an hour. We get to a little diner that looks almost deserted. We go in and find a seat in the corner. I ordered some pie and a drink, and so did Poppy. We wait for about another ten minutes, and a lady I have never seen sits down.

"Ah, you must see the famous River I hear so much about."

"I am, and who might you be?"

"My name is Angel. I work for Mr. Rizzo."

I sit and just look at her. She is tall, taller than myself. Thin, darker skin, I mean dark tan, long dark hair that is curly. Very pretty. She reminds me of an Angel.

She hands over a packet to my Poppy. Shakes his hand and tells him if he needs anything else, to let him know. She gets up to leave.

"Thank you," I whisper. She turns and smiles and leaves. I wonder if I will ever see her again.

Poppy pulls out the contents of the packet. There appears to be a girl around the age of five or six. She looks a lot like me. Long dark hair. Her eye color is different, and she has gray eyes. Or maybe even hazel. There are pictures of her at school and in the park. An older woman and a man are taking her to different places. When I see a face shot of the lady. I have a flashback to the hospital the night she was born. That lady made my Mom sign the papers to give her to them. My Mom had been using it while she was pregnant, and the system would have taken her if they didn't. My Mom signed the papers.

"THAT'S HER!"

"Are you sure, pumpkin?"

"Yeah, that lady was at the hospital the night she was born."

Poppy gets on the phone and calls someone. I can't understand what he is saying. I don't think he is speaking Italian, I think he is speaking a different language.

"Pumpkin, we are sending a team to watch her for now. We have to get Jackson and get to the bottom of this. They will keep their distance for now and watch and make sure she is safe. Her name is Aspen. She lives in a small town in Colorado."

Her name is Aspen. Aw I like that name. I nod and know that it is not safe to move her yet. And truthfully what will I do with a five-year-old anyway.

We get back to the hotel, and I go straight to bed. I am so tired. And pass out.

Over the next few days, I work on finding my brother, but that seems to be more of a challenge. We can't seem to find any leads on that. Maybe there wasn't a brother. Maybe that was made up. I feel sort of lost about all of this.

I was getting restless being in the room and not being able to do anything. I was on the computer when I found some hidden files. But when I click on them, they aren't files. They are cameras.

There are cameras all over the hotel room. Then I click on another one, and there are some at Jazmine's place, Mykayla's place, and even at Zeke's. Plus, I see some for Nick's, Rafael's, and not to mention Shannon's. I found one of the surveillance teams watching over my sister. They have found a way to install cameras in her house. I click on one that has her visible in it.

I watch her play. She was setting up a tea party around her table. Teddy bear sitting and some dolls too. She pours them tea. It is so adorable. I just really, really want to meet her. I wonder if she knows about me.

I spend a lot of time watching her on the computer while the team works on capturing Jackson. I don't want to miss a single minute of her, while I know I can see her. I even found that they installed cameras at her school as well. No one questions me about what I am doing. I know that is because they are just keeping me busy. I remember doing a lot of the stuff she does when I was little. I miss those days. Her Grandma and grandpa play house with her, and have tea parties with her. One day, she even had friends over, and they played with her dolls. I am so in awe of her.

I was watching her play with a little boy. When the door to the room burst open. I clicked to shut it off so no one would know what I was doing. I hear heavy breathing. I wonder what is going on. I look up to see Jazmine breathing hard like she just ran a marathon.

"Are you alright?" I am concerned.

"Water, please." She managed to huff out.

I ran and grabbed some water and handed it to her.

After she catches her breath and is back to breathing normally, I ask her, "What happened?"

"Oh, I had to run here from down the street. I left my car down the block and ran through yards. I didn't want anyone to follow me."

"Why would someone follow you?"

"We got him."

"You got who?"

"Really?"

Oh, it dawned on me. They got Jackson.

Wait, they got Jackson!

"You got him?" I feel some excitement in my body.

"Yeah, we have him at this new warehouse. I had to get the tail to follow me. So Cain and Zeke could get him there. I had to park down the street and take off on foot. Mykayla is taking my car and is going to have them follow her. We, on the other hand, are taking your car and going to head there."

I stare at her with a smile on my face. We got Jackson. Now we can get my life back. Right?

"We don't just stand there, hurry up and get some clothes on."

I rush to my room and put some clothes on, and we take off in my car. Jazmine tells me where to turn so we can get to the warehouse.

When we pull up, my nervousness starts to kick in. We walk in, and I find Cain, Zeke, and Poppy standing around him.

I walk over to him and slap him. "That was for drugging me."

He looks up at me and smirks. "I had no choice. I had to."

"What do you mean you had to? Who are you working for? Why did you send Misty after me? What do I need to do to get my life back? What do you know about me, or my Mom?" I have a zillion and one questions to ask. But I will start with these.

He stares at me for a long time.

"You will not like the answers to those questions." What kind of response is that?

"I have to know."

"I was; I mean, I had to drug you. I was forced to. I was told to drug you and take you to that building. My life was on the line. I didn't send Misty after you. I don't know any Misty. I know a lot about you and your Mom. Way more than you think I know."

"What do I need to do to get my life back? And who are you working for?"

And if Misty wasn't working for him? Who was she working for? Was she working for anyone, or was she just trying to scare me? She did know a lot about me, though.

What shocked me was his response to the person he was working for. My jaw dropped. And I could feel the tears pool up in my eyes, and they ended up overflowing. I could feel the tears running down my cheeks. I wasn't ready for that.

30

Is It Really True?

I am so stunned at what I have just heard from Jackson. I don't believe it's true. I turn around and walk outside. I can hear my name being called, but I don't stop. I run to my car and get in it, and leave. This can't be true. Why does my life have to be so confusing and messed up?

I drive. I drove for a while. I have no idea where I am going, and I probably shouldn't be driving. I should stop and cry. But I have to get far, far away. I need to put distance between me and the world. I need to be alone. I don't know how long I need to be alone, but I do.

I can hear my phone going off, but I don't want to talk to anyone. I am still trying to wrap my mind around the information I was just given. I know if they want to come to me, they can. I mean, they can track my phone. But I am hoping that I can have some space.

I get on the highway where it is flat and hit high speeds. I can still feel the tears pouring down my face and dripping down into my lap. Is there anyone on this planet who is worried about me? Or is everyone out to get me?

I decide I need some music and turn on my music player on my phone. I want the pain I am feeling to just go away. I want to feel better. I want to be a normal eighteen-year-old. Maybe I want to be someone else.

I listen to what comes on. Oh, it makes me sing. It's an angry song. But it will help me feel better.

But you want to justify

Rippin' someone's head off

No human contact

And if you interact

Your life is on contract

Your best bet is to stay away motherfucker

It's just one of those days

I start to get lost in the music playing, and driving, that I lose track of where I am going and what time it is. Truthfully, I am unsure why I am still awake anyway. It has to be from everything I am feeling inside of me right now. I don't even know what to do, or where to begin with the feelings I am having.

My stomach starts to growl. I look at the time and look up to see a sign. Victorville. I pull off the highway, go through a fast-food place, and grab some food. I see a hotel and decide I need to get some sleep. So I pulled into the parking lot. I figured out that I am in California.

I get the room for the rest of the night, plus tomorrow night. I don't want to have to get up in a few hours to drive back. I mean, if I choose to. I get my room key and head up to my room. I thank myself for stashing a bag in the truck just in case. It has a few outfits in it, an extra phone charger, along with a spare laptop.

I get in my room, and it is your typical room. King size bed, a desk with a phone, dresser, a couple of night stands, and a flat screen TV. It isn't as fancy as where I was staying. But I just need to get some sleep. Truthfully, it is nice to be somewhere super fancy. This will be a nice break.

I figured I should let someone know what was going on. I don't want to worry the guys or talk to them right now. I also don't want anyone to show up at the door to gather me back. I need to have time to think about everything that is going on in my head and the whole situation at hand. I sent Gramma and Poppy a message.

Text:

I have checked into a room in California. I need some time to process this. I am OK and will keep in touch with you, so you know I am OK. I am going to sleep.

I don't wait for a reply, but I double-check all the locks on everything to ensure no one can get in. I close my curtains tightly so no one can see that I am in here. Plus, when the sun comes up, I don't want to see it. I want to be able to sleep. I climb into bed and try to go to sleep. Maybe a good night's sleep will make things clearer?

I toss and turn all night long. I keep having nightmares. Nightmares of being killed or traded for drugs. They seem so real, like it is happening to mean. I sort of feel like I am watching it from another view, or like an out-of-body experience is going on. I sleep like crap and I am super glad I can stay right here for as long as I need or want for that matter. I decided to take a hot bath to try and relax. I hope it will help clear my head. Which does help, and I do end up getting some sleep.

When I finally get up, it is already afternoon, and I have to decide if I want to stay longer or if I am ready to go back. I go down to the counter and ask if I can stay a few more nights. They offered me a deal to stay the week for a discounted rate, not that it matters, but I decided to do it. I just need to breathe. I need to sort these things out. I need to figure out myself before I can even begin to deal with anything or anyone else.

I texted Gramma and Poppy to tell them my plan, and they said they understood. I am glad they didn't try to argue with me. Because, honestly, I don't care if they agree or not, I have to do this. I need this time to process everything.

I call my Grandma.

"Grandma, when was the last time you saw Mom?"

"Honey, what is wrong? I haven't seen her since we dropped her off at rehab. I talk to her once a week. Why?"

"Please call the rehab and see if she is there. Call me back when you're done. I love you, and I am going to hang up and do it right away. I need to know."

I hear her say OK and that she loves it. I'm going to go get some food. I get enough to get through the night, so I don't have to leave again. I waited for a while, and still no call back from Grandma. I turn on the TV and watch some comedy that is on. I start to doze off when my phone rings. I jump up, hoping that it is my Grandma, but it isn't.

"Hello, Gramma."

"Dear, I am just letting you know that your Grandma has decided to come to Vegas to visit for a while."

I think about what she says and feel a pain in my gut.

"Did she say why?"

"No, dear, just that she wants to take a vacation. She is going to be getting on a flight in a few days."

I decided that I am going to stay the whole week here. I need my space to re-coop myself and get my bearings. I need to be able to figure things out. I just need to figure it out myself. I need to focus on myself.

"OK, Gramma, I am going to be staying here for at least a week. I need to get some air, and I need some time for myself. Just me for right now. Is that OK?"

"Dear, take all the time you need."

"I love you, Gramma. Tell Poppy I love him too."

"We love you too, dear."

I feel better about my choice to stay. I have to make a list of things I am going to need to get by for the week. I noticed a pool when I checked in, and now I need a swimsuit so I can swim. I need some bathroom stuff. I am feeling hungry, so I head out to get a few things I need from my list and some food.

While I am out, I grab a swimsuit, shampoo, and other beauty products. I also grabbed a couple of big towels. Maybe I will stay here at this hotel for a while longer than a week. I just need time. I don't even know what I want anymore. I grab some writing stuff so I can channel my frustration into writing.

Then I grab some food items. Bottled waters, some soda pop, and a few items that don't need to be kept cold. I am strolling up an aisle, remember when I was a child, my Mom used to buy me cans of Spaghettios. I would eat it right out of the can when Mom would be doped up or out. It was a comfort food for me. So I grab a few cans, maybe it will still comfort me. I just want to go back to when my Daddy was still alive and have him take care of me. Wrap me up in a big bear hug and tell me that everything will be alright.

I feel the tears pooling up in my eyes. I hurried to cash out and get back to my room. I rush in carrying my bags and find my pillow as the tears pour out onto it. Making the pillow wet.

I cry till I cannot cry any longer. I turn over and hear my

stomach growling. I get my food and turn on the TV. I flip through the channels eating my food and I find Rugrats on. I stop. This was my favorite show. My Dad and I used to watch this all the time.

Daddy, I need you to guide me right now. I need to know what to do. I am so lost. I am so confused. My life, it feels like a big fat lie. Why does it have to be me? I am ready to go far, far away and never return. Change my name and get a new life. I don't know who to trust, and I don't know what about my life was the truth and what was a lie.

I finish eating and clean up. I lay back down, still sorting through the thoughts I have in my mind right now. Trying to wrap my fingers and brain around it. I just feel like my whole life is one big fat lie. It was a dozy of a lie. I just don't want to think anymore. I just want my mind to take a break. Tomorrow is a new day. Tomorrow is the day I get my life back. I mean MY LIFE. I am not going to play anyone else's games. I will be playing my own game. I will get the results I want. I only want to have my life back.

Tomorrow brings a new day. A brand new game plan. I will come to terms with how to fix my life. The life my Mom screwed up. The life that I deserve.

I wake up feeling refreshed and jump in the shower. My new life starts today. I put on my swimsuit and head down for a swim and some soaking in the hot tub. While swimming laps, I notice a nice-looking young man jump into the pool. I have a weird feeling, but this is somewhere very populated, and it's not like I am having drinks with him. I continue to swim laps, and notice he starts to swim laps as well. I watch him as I am swimming, and when his strides start to fall in sync with me, I climb out and soak in the hot tub. About ten other people are sitting in there, and there is no room for anyone else, so I feel a bit safe. When people start to get out of the hot tub, I climb out and head to my room. I notice that the guy is watching me.

I lay down after locking my door and take a nap. I end up heading out for dinner. I find a nice quiet little local diner and head in. I ask to be seated at the bar so I am not taking up a table. I ordered a sweet tea and some food. I am waiting for it to be prepared, and the guy from the pool comes in and sits down next to me. Now I am officially worried. I snap a selfie, or at least pretend to, and take one of him. I sent the picture to Zeke.

Text:

Run a check on this guy. I get a creepy feeling about him, and he has been at the pool and is now next to me at dinner. I want to know who he is. And please don't tell the guys I am here or that I made contact with you. Please Zeke.

Text back from Zeke:

You know, for being in love with these guys, you sure are playing some messed-up mind games. They are going stir crazy. I am already running the pic you have sent me. I won't tell them you sent me a text. But they will be made that I didn't. I understand you need some time to clear that mind because of that effed up stuff Jackson said. But remember, you have us to lean on if you want us. I will drive there tonight and stay with you. So will any of us.

I have an awe moment when he says he will come stay with me. But did he say that I love the guys? I never said that, did I?

Text back to Zeke:

I never said I loved the guys. And thank you, if I need company, I will let you know. Let me know what you find out.

Ping back to me:

You didn't have to say it. I can see it in your eyes. Night River.

Can he tell from just looking in my eyes? Does everyone else know what is going on based on my eyes? I am staring at my phone when I hear someone talking to me. I zoned out.

"Must be some conversation you're having."

I turn and see that the guy is trying to talk to me.

"Yes, yes, it is."

I leave it vague, hoping he would leave it alone and move on to the next girl. I am not interested.

"Was that your boyfriend?"

I know it wasn't, but I told him yes anyway.

"The fool is crazy for letting you out of the house without him. I would be sitting at home, jealous of other guys. Someone else might come in and scoop you up."

Really? Did he really just say that? Am I ice cream?

"First off, I am not ice cream. You cannot come in and scoop me up. Or anyone else, for that matter. Second thing, he didn't let me out. I let myself out. My boyfriend doesn't control me. I am my OWN person. Third, you need to learn how to treat a lady, like a lady, starting with how you talk to them. Enjoy your dinner." I ask for my food to go and pay the bill. I pay it and I turn and leave.

I am very steamed off now, and didn't want to be sitting next to that jerk. I can feel the blood in my body begin to boil. Maybe staying here was a bad idea. I think I want to go to the ocean. I pull up the laptop and look up at a coastal hotel. I want to see the ocean, something I have never done. Then I remember I never made a bucket list. I need to do that too.

List:

See the ocean.

Meet my sister.

Meet my brother.

Get my life back.

Go to Europe.

See the Hollywood sign.

That is a good start, and I can cross off two real soon. I find a hotel and figure out I am only a few hours away from it. I throw my stuff into my bag and jump in my car. I didn't check out, because I want people to think I am still there. I drive to Malibu and check into a king suite with a view of the ocean. It is already dark, so I can't go out and stand in the ocean, but the moonlight over it makes it beautiful. I sit on the balcony and just enjoy the warmth. I let Poppy know where I am and that the creepy guy made me want to leave. I am starting to feel better, and I know that after I cross off the Hollywood sign, I need to head back and lay out a new plan. Maybe I need to move around a bit. But not before we fix the biggest issue at hand. The real reason I am on the run.

I make my way back into the room and crash. I can't even keep my eyes open any longer. I woke up in time to see the sunrise over the ocean. It is the most beautiful thing I have ever seen in my life. I am so mesmerized by the view that I don't even notice my stomach growling. I have to go into the ocean. I grab my suit, stick it on, grab some jean shorts and a tank top, and head down for breakfast on the beach. I eat and step into the water. This is so awesome. I take some selfies when I notice that guy from the other hotel. OK, not gonna lie, I am freaked out now. Maybe it is time to deal with the issue at hand and head home.

I gather up my stuff and head back to the room. I feel someone grab my arm, and I turn and swing and connect to someone's jaw. They let go, and I took off running. I make it to my room and lock the door. I run and shut the slider and lock it too. I start to panic.

I call Poppy. I tell him what is going on, and he tells me to stay put. Not to leave the room for any reason. I am getting so freaking scared. I was watching out the peephole, and I could see that guy from the other hotel talking to some other people. I can't hear what they are saying, but I can see him. They all leave the hallway and go further down. I moved the furniture in front of the door just in case. I curl up in a ball, rocking back and forth. What seemed like hours, but in reality it was only like twenty minutes, I jumped. I listen. I can hear Cain's voice. No, that is not even possible. I mean, he is in Vegas, not Malibu.

My phone rings. I pick it up and hear Poppy tell me to open the door. So I do, and it is Cain. He comes in, grabs me, and picks me up, and I lose it. I start crying and I say that I am so sorry for everything. But all I needed was time. He tells me it's OK and helps me gather my stuff. We check out and get into my car to drive home. I don't even ask how he got there so quickly, but I am assuming he was nearby. Leave it to my guys to be near to keep me safe even when I don't want it.

I fall asleep while Cain drives. The next thing I know, we are pulling in at home, back in Vegas. He wakes me up and we head inside.

I walk inside. I am brought into a hug by all my guys. Which once again brings tears to my eyes. How could I be so selfish? I was so worried about myself that I didn't care about what I had been hurting because they care so much about me. They let go just so I could get hugs from my grandparents, all three of them.

I walked into the living room and sat down on the couch.

"So, your Grandma has given us some very interesting news." I turn to look at Poppy. "Your Mom checked herself out seventy-two hours after being admitted. We have no location for her. We have every team we can spare searching for some sort of lead in her location. At this point, we are unsure who is after you. If it's Roman, Felix, or your Mom. But the numbers in contact with Jackson are not known numbers to be connected to Roman or Felix. We have Jackson still in custody, and his phone is on, waiting for the next contact to be made so we can find Rosalie. I am so sorry that this is happening to you. We haven't made a move on your sister yet because she still doesn't know where she is, and if we move, she will find her."

I take a deep breath. So it is true. My Mom is after me. I keep breathing deeply. My Mom is after me. Why is my Mom after me? I can't believe it. I feel the tears running down my face as the truth sets in.

My Mom is REALLY after me.

About the Author

Everly is an author and mother. She has one daughter and one son biologically along with 3 bonus kids whom she loves as if they were her own. Her husband and her met online and fell in love on their first date. Everly has been writing since she was a young girl and after many years of self doubt she has decided to take the jump into publishing to see if other people love her story and her characters as much as she does.